Best Friends

I wonder if you've ever lost your best friend? The friend you've know ever since you were little, the friend that's closer than a sister, more fun than any brother? Maybe she lives on the other side of town now and goes to a different school. Maybe she's moved right away to a different part of the country and you can't even meet up at weekends and in the holidays. Maybe your best friend is still living nearby but you've had a quarrel and she's gone off with another girl now and she won't even speak to you.

Grown-ups often don't understand how devastating this can be. Even the kindest mums and dads will just give you a quick cuddle and then say, 'Well, cheer up, you'll find a new best friend in next to no time.'

Sometimes, wonderfully, they're right. A new girl comes to the school and you hit it off straight away and within weeks you're doing your homework together and confiding all sorts of secrets and having sleepovers at each other's houses.

But sometimes grown-ups can be 100 per cent wrong. It isn't always easy to find a new best friend.

Everyone at their school has their own circle of friends and you can't just barge in and be part of the gang. Someone might be especially kind and try hard to be friendly, but maybe you don't like them much. They're not the same as your old best friend.

I tried to write about this situation as truthfully as possible in *Best Friends* – but I promise this isn't a sad book. There are lots of really funny bits. My all-time favourite boy character Biscuits pops up in this story. I loved writing about him in *Cliffhanger* and *Buried Alive*. He's such a cheerful, good-hearted boy – and we discover in *Best Friends* that he can make wonderful cakes, too!

But this is really the story of Gemma and Alice, best friends since the day they were born. Shall I tell you how I got their names? One day at a big book signing, two little girls came up to me and announced together: 'We're best friends.'

'I'm just about to start writing a story about best friends,' I said. 'I haven't chosen their names yet. What are you two called?'

'Gemma and Alice,' they said.

'OK, that's what I'll call the girls in my new book,' I said, and I kept my promise.

I do hope the real Gemma and Alice have read the book. I also hope they're still best friends!

Jacqueline Wilson

Best Friends

Jacqueline Wilson

Illustrated by Nick Sharratt

CORGI YEARLING

BEST FRIENDS

A CORGI YEARLING BOOK 978 0 440 87228 3

First published in Great Britain by Doubleday,
an imprint of Random House Children's Publishers UK

Doubleday edition published 2004
First Corgi Yearling edition published 2005
This Corgi Yearling edition published 2008

022

Penguin Random House is committed to a sustainable future for
our business, our readers and our planet. This book is made from
Forest Stewardship Council® certified paper.

MIX
Paper from
responsible sources
FSC® C018179

Printed and bound in Great Britain by Clays Ltd, Elcograf S.p.A.

Corgi Yearling Books are published by Random House Children's Publishers UK,
61–63 Uxbridge Road, London W5 5SA

www.randomhousechildrens.co.uk
www.randomhouse.co.uk

Addresses for companies within The Random House Group Limited can be found at:
www.randomhouse.co.uk/offices.htm

THE RANDOM HOUSE GROUP Limited Reg. No. 954009

A CIP catalogue record for this book is available from the British Library.

For Scarlett, Fergus and Phoebe

One

Alice and I are best friends. I've known her all my life. That is absolutely true. Our mums were in hospital at the same time when they were having us. I got born first, at six o'clock in the morning on 3 July. Alice took ages and didn't arrive until four in the afternoon. We both had a long cuddle with our mums and at night time we were tucked up next to each other in little weeny cots.

I expect Alice was a bit frightened. She'd have cried. She's actually still a bit of a crybaby now but I try not to tease her about it. I always do my best to comfort her.

I bet that first day I called to her in baby-coo language. I'd say, 'Hi, I'm Gemma. Being born is a bit weird, isn't it? Are you OK?'

And Alice would say, 'I'm not sure. I'm Alice. I don't think I like it here. I want my mum.'

'We'll see our mums again soon. We'll get fed.

7

I'm *starving*.' I'd have started crying too, in case there was a chance of being fed straight away.

I suppose I'm still a bit greedy, if I'm absolutely honest. Not quite as greedy as Biscuits though. Well, his real name is Billy McVitie, but everyone calls him Biscuits, even the teachers. He's this boy in our class at school and his appetite is astonishing. He can eat an entire packet of chocolate Hob Nobs, munch crunch, munch crunch, in two minutes flat.

We had this Grand Biscuit Challenge at play time. I only managed three quarters of a packet. I probably could have managed a whole packet too but a crumb went down the wrong way and I choked. I ended up with chocolate biscuit drool all down the front of my white school blouse. But that's nothing new. I always seem to get a bit messy and scruffy and scuffed. Alice stays neat and sweet.

When we were babies *one* of us crawled right into the rubbish bin and played mud wrestling in the garden and fell in the pond when we fed the ducks. The *other* one of us sat up prettily in her buggy cuddling Golden Syrup (her yellow teddy bear) and giggled at her naughty friend.

When we went to nursery school *one* of us played Fireman in the water tank and Moles in the sand tray, and she didn't stop at Finger Painting, she did Entire Body Painting. The

other one of us sat demurely at the dinky table and made plasticine necklaces (one for each of us) and sang 'Incy Wincy Spider' with all the cute hand gestures.

When we went to infants school *one* of us pretended to be a Wild Thing and roared such terrible roars in class she got sent out of the room. She also got into a fight with a big boy who snatched her best friend's chocolate and *made his nose bleed*! The *other* one of us read *Milly-Molly-Mandy* and wrote stories about a little thatched cottage in the country in her very neat printing.

Now we're in the juniors *one* of us ran right into the boys' toilets for a dare. She did, really, and they all yelled at her. She also climbed halfway up the drainpipe in the playground to get her ball back – only the drainpipe came away from the wall. They both went *crash clonk*. Mr Beaton the headteacher was NOT pleased. The *other* one of us got made a form monitor and wore her silver sparkly top to the school disco (with matching silver glitter on her eyelids) and all the boys wanted to dance with her, but *guess what*! She danced with her bad best friend all evening instead.

We're best friends but we're not one bit alike. I suppose that goes without saying. Though I seem to have said it a lot. My mum says it too. Also a lot.

'For heaven's sake, Gemma, why can't you stop being so rough and silly and boisterous? *Boy* being the operative bit! To think I was so thrilled when I had my baby girl. But now it's just like I've got three boys – and you're the biggest tearaway of them all!'

There's my big brother Callum who's seventeen. Callum and I used to be mates. He taught me to skateboard and showed me how to dive-bomb in the swimming baths. Every Sunday I'd balance on the back of his bike and we'd wobble over to Grandad's. But now Callum's got this girlfriend Ayesha and all they do is look into each other's eyes and go kissy-kissy-kiss. Yuck.

Alice and I played spies and followed them to the park once because we wanted to see if they did anything even yuckier but Callum caught us and he turned me upside down and shoogled me until I felt sick.

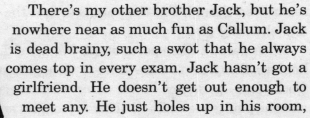

There's my other brother Jack, but he's nowhere near as much fun as Callum. Jack is dead brainy, such a swot that he always comes top in every exam. Jack hasn't got a girlfriend. He doesn't get out enough to meet any. He just holes up in his room, hunched over his home-work. He *does* take our dog Barking Mad out for a walk very late at night. And he likes to wear black. And doesn't like garlic bread. Maybe Jack is turning into Jacula? I'll have to check his teeth aren't getting alarmingly pointy.

It's annoying having Jack as my brother. Sometimes the teachers hope I'm going to be dead brainy too and get ten out of ten all the time. As if!

I can do *some* things. Mr Beaton says I can talk the hind leg off a donkey – and its front leg and its ears and its tail. He says I *act* like a donkey too. I think donkeys kick if you're not careful. I *often* feel like kicking Mr Beaton.

I get lots of ideas and work things out as quick as quick in my head but it's soooo boring writing it all down so I often don't bother. Or I try to get Alice to write it all out for me. Alice gets much better marks than me for all lessons. Apart from football. I don't want to boast but I'm in the school football team even though I'm the youngest and the littlest and the only girl.

Alice doesn't like sports at all. We have different hobbies. She likes to draw lines of little girls in party frocks and she writes in her diary with her gel pens and she paints her nails all different colours and plays with her jewellery. Alice is into jewellery in a big way. She keeps it in a special box that used to be her grandma's. It's blue velvet and if you wind it up and open the lid a little ballet dancer twirls round and round. Alice has got a little gold heart on a chain and a tiny gold bangle she wore when she was a baby and a jade bangle from an uncle in Hong Kong and a silver locket and a Scottie dog sparkly brooch and a charm bracelet with ten jingly charms. My favourite charm is the little silver Noah's Ark. You can open it up and see absolutely minute giraffes and elephants and tigers inside.

Alice also has heaps of rings – a real Russian gold ring, a Victorian garnet and lots of pretendy ones out of crackers. She gave me a big bright silver and blue one as a friendship ring. I loved it and called it my sapphire – only I forgot to take it off when I went swimming and the silver went black and the sapphire fell out.

'Typical,' said Mum, sighing.

I think Mum sometimes wishes she'd swapped

12

the cots round when we were born. I'm sure she'd much rather have Alice as a daughter. She doesn't say so, but I'm not daft. *I'd* sooner have Alice as my daughter.

'I wouldn't,' said my dad, and he ruffled my hair so it stood up on end. Well, it was probably standing up anyway. I've got the sort of hair that looks like I'm permanently plugged into the electrics. Mum made me grow it long but I kept losing my silly bows and bobbles. Then it got a bit sticky when I went in for this giant bubble-blowing contest with Biscuits and the other boys and *hurray hurray* my hair had to be chopped off. Mum cried but I didn't mind one bit.

I know you're not really meant to have favourites in your family but I think I love my dad more than my mum. I don't get to see him much because he drives a taxi and so he's up before I wake up, taking people to the airport, and often he's out till very late picking people up from the pub. When he *is* home he likes to lie on the sofa in front of the telly and have a little snooze. It's often a long long long snooze, but if you're feeling lonely you can cuddle up beside him. He pats you and mumbles, 'Hello, little Cuddle Bun,' and then goes back to sleep again.

My grandad used to drive our cab but he's retired now, though he helps out when the car hire firm need an extra driver. They've got a white Rolls for weddings and Grandad once took me for a sneaky drive in it. He's lovely, my grandad. Maybe he's my all-time absolute *favourite* relative. He's always looked after me, right from when I was a baby. Our mum went back to work full time just as Grandad retired so he's acted like my child minder.

He still meets me from school. We go back to Grandad's flat, which is right at the top of the tower block. You look out of Grandad's window and you see the birds flying past, it's just magical. On a clear day you can see for miles and miles across the town to the woods and hills of the countryside. Sometimes Grandad narrows his eyes and pretends he's looking through a telescope. He swears he's squinting all the way to the sea, but I think he's joking.

He jokes a lot, my grandad. He calls me funny names too. I'm his little Iced Gem. He always gives me packets of iced gems, small doll-size biscuits with white and pink and yellow yummy icing.

This annoys Mum when she collects me. 'I wish you wouldn't feed her,' she says to Grandad, 'she's going to have her tea the minute she gets home. Gemma, you mind you clean your teeth properly. I don't like you eating all that sugary stuff.'

Grandad always says he's sorry but he crosses his eyes behind Mum's back and pulls a funny face. I get the giggles and annoy Mum even more.

Sometimes I think *everyone* annoys my mum. Everyone except Alice. Mum works in the make-up department of Joseph Pilbeam, the big store, and she gives Alice all these dinky samples of skincare products, and little lipsticks and bottles of scent. Once when she was in a really good mood she sat Alice down at her dressing table and gave her a full grown-up lady's make-up. My mum made me up too, though she told me off for fidgeting (well, it was tickly) and then my eyes itched and I rubbed them and got that black mascara stuff all over the place so I looked like a panda.

Alice's make-up stayed prettily in place all day long. She didn't even smudge her pink lipstick when she had her tea. It was pizza, but she cut hers up into tiny bite-size pieces instead of shoving a lovely big wedge in her mouth.

If Alice wasn't my very best friend she might just get on my nerves sometimes. Especially when Mum makes a big fuss of her and then looks at me and sighs.

15

Still, it's great that Mum *does* like Alice because she never minds if she comes for a sleepover at our house. My mum has banned big birthday sleepovers for ever. Callum doesn't care as the only person he'd like to sleep over is Ayesha. Jack doesn't care either. He's got a few nerdy swotty friends in Year Nine but they don't communicate face to face, they just e-mail and text each other.

I've got heaps of ordinary friends as well as my best friend Alice. Last birthday I invited three boys and three girls for a sleepover party. Alice was top of the list, of course. We were supposed to play out in the garden but it rained, so we all had a crazy game of football with a cushion in the living room (well, not quite *all* – Alice wouldn't play and Biscuits is rubbish at games). Someone broke my mum's wedding present Lladro lady *and* burst the cushion. My mum was so mad she wouldn't let any of them sleep over and sent them all home. Except for Alice.

I'm still allowed one-special-friend sleepovers so long as that special friend is Alice. So that's great great great because as I've probably said before, Alice is my very best friend.

I don't know what I'd do without her.

Two

I don't know what to do. I'm worried. Something weird is going on.

It's Alice. She's got a secret and she's not telling me. We've never ever had secrets from each other before.

I've told Alice all sorts of stuff. Even dead embarrassing awful things, like the time I *thought* I could make it home from McDonald's after drinking two large Cokes and a milkshake without going to the loo. Alice knows I don't like to sleep without my little rabbit-house night-light because I don't actually like the dark very much. When Grandad had to go into hospital for an operation I told Alice I was scared he wouldn't get better, though thank goodness he was fine again in no time.

Alice has always told me her secret stuff too. She told me when her mum and dad had a big row because her dad drank too much at a party. She told me how she once stole a chocolate toffee from the video shop.

It was on the floor so she hoped it might count as rubbish but she was still scared it meant she was a thief. She was so worried about it she didn't even dare eat the toffee. I ate it for her, just so she'd stop worrying about it.

She's told me heaps and heaps of stuff. But now she's got this secret. She doesn't know that *I* know she's got a secret. I found out in a bad way. I read her diary.

I know you shouldn't ever read anyone's private diary. Especially not your best friend's. I've actually had a peep at Alice's diary several times. Not to be mean and sneaky. It's just so interesting finding out what she's thinking, like there's a little window in her forehead and you can peep through into her brain. It's usually lovely because she writes all this stuff about *me*.

Gemma was so funny in class today that even Mrs Watson burst out laughing . . . Gemma and I made up our own cartoon story about all the animals in Noah's Ark and the giraffes stood up too suddenly and made a hole in the roof and it was raining hard but the elephants spread their ears to keep Noah and his family dry. Gem gets such *good* ideas . . .

18

I was feeling fed up at school today because Mum won't let me have that suede jacket we saw on Saturday but Gemma shared her chocolate with me and said she'll buy me as many suede jackets as I want when we're grown up.

I love it that she writes page after page saying I'm comical and inventive and kind. I love it that she's stuck a funny photo of us with our arms round each other at the front of her diary. She's outlined it with silver pen like it's a frame and then stuck her favourite stickers of flowers and dolphins and kittens and ballet dancers all over the page.

This is why I took the tiniest peek at her diary yesterday. We'd had a lovely afternoon making a picture of the flat we're going to share together when we're old enough. Alice seemed a little odd about this at first, but I just thought it was because she's not quite as good at drawing as I am.

She perked up when I said we'd cut stuff out of my mum's magazines. She liked choosing and cutting out our twin beds and our huge squashy velvet sofa and our giant fridge and our big white furry rug. She started cutting weeny bright hexagons out of the magazines in different colours to make into patchwork quilts for our beds, with matching patchwork cushions for the sofa. I enjoyed cutting out lots of food to stick into our fridge, although some of the tubs of ice cream and chocolate éclairs were so big they spilled out onto the floor. Imagine a tub of ice cream so big you could stick your whole head inside it to have a good lick; imagine chocolate éclairs so enormous you could sit astride them (though it might make your knickers a bit sticky). Then I inked eyes and ears and a snout and four claws on the big white furry rug, turning it into a real live polar bear for us to cuddle and take turns riding on his back.

Alice *did* get a bit irritated about that. 'I thought we were going to do this properly, Gem. You're just messing about,' she said, opening and closing her little pink mouth every time she opened and closed her scissors.

I got a bit irritated too because she spent ages and ages getting all the colours of her patchwork pieces in place and making them into a pattern. Alice got even more irritated when I had an itchy nose and sneezed and blew all the pieces about before she'd had a chance to stick them down.

But that was just *us*, ordinary Alice-and-Gemma fuss. It wasn't like a real quarrel. We don't ever ever ever have proper quarrels. We haven't ever broken friends, not even for half a day. *So why won't she tell me this terrible secret?*

Doesn't she want me to be her friend any more? She did act a bit weird at tea time. It was a special tea, even though it was just Mum and Alice and me. Dad was out in his cab working, Callum was round at Ayesha's and Jack had a tray up in his room because he couldn't be dragged away from his computer. We had Mum's spag bol and then fruit salad with that lovely squirty whippy cream out of a can and *then* a handful of Smarties each. I chose all the blue ones and Alice picked out all the pink.

I ate everything up. In fact I even licked my plate when Mum wasn't watching. Alice didn't eat much at all. She's usually a *bit* picky about her food, but she loves spag bol and fruit and cream and Smarties as much as me, so this was definitely a bad sign. She didn't even want to have a who-can-suck-up-her-spaghetti-fastest competition. When my plate was totally empty Alice was still winding her spaghetti round and round her fork in a thoughtful way, but not actually *eating* it.

'I'll eat yours if you like,' I offered, just to be helpful.

'You leave Alice's plate alone, Gemma!' said Mum. 'Just because you hoover yours up in two

21

minutes flat! Honestly, you've got the table manners of a starving gorilla.'

I started monkeying around then, beating my chest and smacking my lips, until Mum got cross, which wasn't really *fair* because she'd started the gorilla reference. Alice's spag bol was stone cold by this time so Mum tactfully removed it. Alice did eat a little fruit salad, though she just pressed one weeny dollop of cream on top. I seriously sprayed my plate, making a cream mountain, until Mum snatched the can away.

Then we had the Smarties.

'Remember we had Smarties stuck all round the icing on our last birthday cake?' I said. 'Hey, did you know you get a special wish every seventh Smartie?'

'No you don't. You just made that up. You only get wishes when you cut your birthday cake,' said Alice. 'We haven't got a cake. And it isn't our birthday.'

'We can make a wish any time we want, birthdays or *un*birthdays. Come on, Alice, wish with me.'

We always wish the same wish.

'We wish we stay friends for ever and ever and ever,' I said.

I dug Alice in the ribs with my elbow and then she said it too. Mumbling a little. Then she ducked her head and had a drink of juice. She coughed and spluttered and had to run to the bathroom.

'Oh dear, poor Alice. Did she choke on a Smartie?' said Mum.

'I don't think so,' I said.

When she came back from the bathroom Alice's eyes were all red. I know your eyes water a bit if you choke. But she looked as if she'd been crying.

I didn't think too much of it at the time. Alice *is* a bit of a crybaby. She cries at the most ridiculous things. She even cries when she's happy, like the time I gave her my grandma's china doll, Melissa. She left her to me when she died. I loved her because she was my grandma's special doll. She'd been *her* grandma's special doll once upon a time. Melissa was very pretty, with soft brown ringlets and shiny brown eyes with proper eyelashes. I liked flicking her eyelids up and down, making her blink very realistically. Mum got narked and said I'd poke Melissa's eyes out if I wasn't careful.

Alice loved my doll too, especially her beautiful white dress and petticoats and her long lacy knickers (imagine wearing knickers way past your knees!). I really really wanted Melissa to play with. I'm not at all a girly girl but I've always liked playing games with dolls. Wild, messy, exciting games. My Barbies trekked through garden jungles and wrestled with earthworms and nearly drowned in torrential rain.

I looked at pristine Melissa. Even her little pearl-buttoned suede boots were white. I knew just what she'd look like if I kept her. I suddenly knew what to do. I gave Melissa to Alice. Alice clasped her to her chest (carefully, so her clothes weren't crushed) and great fat tears spurted down her cheeks.

I got worried in case I'd made a mistake and she didn't really like Melissa. Alice insisted she was crying for joy. I cried tears of anguish, fury and despair later that day when Mum found out. She was sooooo cross with me for giving away Grandma's doll.

I wondered if Alice could possibly have been crying tears of joy because of our special Smartie wish but this seemed a little excessive, even for Alice.

She seemed fine again after tea. We watched television together, and when our favourite pop programme came on we sang along too and did all the dance routines. Well, Alice danced every step correctly; I just jumped up and down and waved my arms around.

Callum came and joined in for a bit. He dances even more wildly than me. Alice gets a bit

24

nervous when he does his crazy jive stuff and flings us about, but I love it. Then Callum rushed off round to see Ayesha.

Alice and I took Barking Mad for a run round the garden. We had one more go at training him to do tricks. When he was a little fluffy puppy he'd hold out his paw and shake it in this seriously cute way. I got terribly excited and thought we could train him up to be a performing Wonder Dog. Alice and I could be part of the act. I could wear a top hat and tails and give Barking Mad his orders. Alice could wear a frilly ballet frock and be my number one assistant.

However, Barking Mad *went* barking mad when he got to be a teenager. He wouldn't do any tricks at all. He'd occasionally shake paws if he was in a very good mood and you bribed him with chocolate, but he absolutely refused to dance on his hind legs or turn somersaults or bark happy birthday. He'd *bark*, all right, very loudly and persistently, telling you to woof off and stop pestering him.

WOOF WOOF GRRR!!

He did that last night when I tried to get him to balance on a flowerpot. It was a *big* flowerpot. He could have done it easy-peasy if he'd wanted. But he didn't want. He got so cross about it that Jack unchained himself from his computer and came stumbling down from his bedroom to rescue him.

'Leave him be, you little dog torturer,' he said, hauling Barking Mad away.

'I'm simply trying to help him achieve stardom,' I said. 'I've even thought of a professional name for him. The Dog Star. Do you get it? There's a *real* Dog Star—'

'And I wish you'd swoop off and live on it,' said Jack, dragging Barking Mad back to the house.

I mouthed rude words behind his back. Alice giggled. Then we climbed up onto the big branch of the apple tree and traded all the really rude words we knew. I know *heaps* more than Alice. It was great dangling our legs from the branch. I tried bouncing up and down a bit but Alice got scared. Then she said she had pins and needles in her bottom and wanted to get down. So we did.

Dad's been promising to make me a proper tree house for ages and ages but he never seems to have time to get so much as started on it. I know Alice would *love* a tree house.

Then Mum called us indoors and we got ready for bed. We sat in our pyjamas at either end of my bed with a big bowl of popcorn between us. I played at being a sea lion, throwing pieces of popcorn up in the air and catching them in my mouth, while Alice wrote her diary. I wasn't always a very *efficient* sea lion, though I did my best.

'You keep jogging me, leaping about like that,' said Alice.

'Well, it's difficult, catching popcorn,' I said, munching.

'You'll choke if you're not careful,' said Alice, closing her diary. 'Stop being so piggly, Gem. I want to put nail varnish on now. Come on, I'll do your nails too.'

'Boring,' I said. 'You'll just nag at me for smudging them.'

'So *don't* smudge them,' said Alice sternly. She reached for her nail varnish pot and opened it.

'You sound just like my mum sometimes,' I said, nudging her with my toes.

I nudged her a little too enthusiastically. I knocked the big bowl so popcorn exploded all over the bed. Alice jumped and spilled pink gloopy nail varnish all over her wrist and up her pyjama sleeve.

'Oh *Gem*!' she shrieked. She jumped up and went to the bathroom to try to wipe it off.

I did my best to scoop popcorn back into the bowl. It had wriggled its way into everything, even crack-

27

ling inside Alice's diary. I shook it out – and then had a little weeny glance at what she'd written.

Then I read it again. And again.

I don't know what to do. I feel so awful. I can't tell Gemma. I simply can't. It has to stay a SECRET. Yet it's so hard to act like normal, as if we're going to carry on in the same old way, like Gemma wished, best friends for ever.

Has Alice got a *new* best friend?

Has she simply got sick of me?

I couldn't sleep. I wriggled around miserably in the popcorn crumbs, wondering whether to wake Alice up and ask her outright. In the end I just cuddled up close to her. I twined a lock of her long hair round and round my fingers, as if I was tying her to me for ever.

Three

I didn't say a word about the Secret when we woke up. Alice didn't either.

I didn't say a word about the Secret when we went downstairs and fixed ourselves great big bowls of Frosties with extra sugar and a handful of sultanas, and those little hundreds-and-thousands cake sprinkles to make rainbow milk. Alice didn't either.

I didn't say a word about the Secret when we watched television. Alice didn't either.

I didn't say a word about the Secret when we acted out our favourite television programme *The Story of Tracy Beaker*. Alice didn't either.

Alice hardly said anything at all, even when she was pretending to be Louise or Justine or Elaine the Pain (I always play Tracy). Still, Alice is always much quieter than me.

I wasn't quiet. The more scared I get inside the noisier I get on the outside. Noisier and noisier, till Mum came rushing downstairs in her dressing gown, very cross.

'For heaven's sake, Gemma, stop that shrieking! Your dad didn't get home till two this morning.'

'I'm being Tracy Beaker, Mum. I've got to shriek. And stamp. And kick. And whirl about,' I said, demonstrating.

Mum seized hold of me. 'Will you *stop* it!' She gave me a little shake. Mum never smacks me but I think she often *wants* to. She rolled her eyes at Alice. 'Why do you *like* being friends with our Gemma?'

'I don't know, Auntie Liz. I just do,' said Alice – and then she burst into tears.

'Oh darling, don't cry!' said Mum. 'I'm not cross with *you*.'

'I don't want you to be cross with Gemma either,' Alice wept.

'Well, I'm not really *cross*. Just a little bit agitated. I'm afraid that's a permanent state round our Gemma,' said Mum. She ruffled my hair ruefully. 'Look at you, Gem! Your hair's sticking straight up like a lavatory brush.'

'Well please don't shove me down the toilet, Mum,' I said.

Mum was busy mopping Alice's face with kitchen towel. Alice usually cries just a little bit, tears delicately dripping down her pink cheeks. But now it was as if she'd sprung a leak: tears spurted, her nose ran, her mouth dribbled. She looked almost ugly, utterly unlike Alice.

'Oh please don't cry, Alice,' I said. I hugged her and started howling myself.

'Oh for heaven's sake,' said Mum. 'You girls! Don't be so silly. I give up. There's nothing to cry about.' She flicked us both lightly on our runny noses with the towel and then went upstairs to the bathroom.

I looked at Alice. She looked at me. I gave a huge sniff and wiped my nose with the back of my hand.

'Yuck,' said Alice. She got some kitchen towel and blew delicately. 'Gem,' she said, in a sad little whisper. 'Gem, there *is* something to cry about.'

'I thought there might be,' I said. I felt as if I was standing on Grandad's window ledge, about to be pushed out into great grey emptiness.

'I don't know how to tell you,' said Alice.

'Just spit it out,' I said, touching her lips, trying to make her mouth move. She pretended to bite my fingers.

'I'm not very good at spitting. Unlike you,' she said. (I had once been the undisputed champion of the splashiest spit competition held behind the bike sheds at school.)

We both giggled feebly even though we were still crying.

31

'Shall I spit it out for you? You don't want to be my best friend any more,' I said.

'No, it's not that!' said Alice, but she looked stricken.

'It's OK. Well, it's not one *bit* OK, but I do understand. I'm not sure *I'd* want to be my best friend. I'm noisy and silly and messy and I break things and I get on everyone's nerves.'

'You don't get on *my* nerves. I want you to be my best friend for ever and ever, only . . . only . . .'

'Only what? What *is* this great big secret, Alice? Come on, you've got to tell me.'

'How do you know there's a secret?'

'Look, I'm ever so sorry and I know it's a totally sneaky thing to do and you really *won't* want to be friends with me now, but I read your diary. Just a line or two. Last night. Well, maybe I've had one or two peeps in the past but you never wrote anything *secret* before—'

 'Gem, stop burbling,' said Alice. She took hold of my hand. 'I *do* still want to be friends. Though don't you dare read my diary again, you nosy pig! But I swore to my mum and dad that I wouldn't tell anyone, not even you, not till it was all settled. But you'll find out soon enough anyway. The thing is, I think we're moving.'

'You're moving?' I said. I felt as if the tightest belt in the world had suddenly unbuckled and set my tummy free. 'Is that all? Oh Alice, that's OK. *Where* are you moving? Don't worry, if it's right the other side of town I'll get Dad to give me a lift to your new place in the taxi – it couldn't be simpler.'

'We're moving to Scotland,' said Alice.

'Scotland? But that's hundreds of miles away!'

She could just as easily have said Timbuktu. Or the Gobi Desert. Or Mars. The belt rebuckled, tightening until I could barely breathe.

'But how will I see you?'

'I know, I know, it's so awful, isn't it,' said Alice, crying again.

'What about school?'

'I've got to go to a new school and I won't know anyone. I won't have any friends,' Alice wailed.

'But *why* are you going?'

'My dad's getting a new job with this Scottish firm and my mum wants to live up there because we'll be able to get a bigger house. And we're going to have a huge garden and Mum says I can have a swing and a tree house.'

'*I'm* going to have a tree house, you know I am, when Dad gets round to it,' I said. 'It was going to be *our* tree house.'

'And I can have any pets I want.'

'You've got a share of Barking Mad.'

'Mum said I can maybe have my own pony.'

I was brought up short. 'A pony!' I'd always longed and longed to have a pony. When I was very little I used to hold my hands up like I was holding reins and I'd gallop along, pretending I was riding this fantasy white horse Diamond. Well, you call white horses grey but Diamond was as white as snow and sometimes he grew wings like Pegasus and we flew up and over the town until we got to the sea and then we'd gallop for hours, skimming the waves.

I stared at Alice. 'Are you *really* getting a pony?'

'Well, Mum said I could. And Dad, though he didn't promise. It's still not definite we're going. Dad hasn't been given a starting time for his job and we haven't completed some contract thingy with the house so we're not telling anyone yet.'

'But I'm not *anyone*. I'm your best friend! *Why* did you keep it a secret from me? I would have *had* to tell you or I'd burst!'

'Yes, I know, Gem. That's why. You'd have told heaps of people because you can't ever keep secrets.'

'I can! Well, sometimes I can. Anyway, why does it have to be this great big secret?'

'We're not telling people till the last minute because my gran and grandad will go nuts and try

34

to stop us.'

I was shocked. 'You mean you're leaving them behind?'

'Well, Dad says we've got no option,' said Alice.

I couldn't ever imagine leaving Grandad behind. I'd sooner leave Mum and Dad than Grandad. But I'd leave all three if it meant I could stay with Alice.

'You're leaving me behind too,' I said.

Alice's face crumpled. 'I don't know how I'm going to bear it, Gemma. I told Mum and Dad I couldn't go because I'd miss you too much. They just laughed at me and said I'd make some new friends – but I don't want any new friends. I just want you.'

'You've still *got* me. We can still be best friends. And tell you what, I'll come and visit you every weekend! I'll get the train,' I said, getting excited.

'You can't, Gem. It takes hours and hours and hours and it costs heaps and heaps too.'

'More than two pounds for a child fare?' I said. I got two pounds pocket money every week. Well, in theory I did. It depended on whether I'd been naughty or cheeky or broken anything. I resolved to behave like Little Miss Perfection from now on.

But it was no use.

'It's forty-eight pounds.'

'What!'

'And that's a supersaver price.'

35

I'd need to save for nearly six months for just one visit.

'What are we going to do?' I cried.

'We can't do anything. We're just children. We don't count,' said Alice bitterly.

'Well, you did say it's not *definite* definite. Maybe your dad won't get the job after all. And they'll sell the house to some other family. And you'll stay here, where you belong. With me.' I said it very fiercely and firmly, as if I could make it true just by being insistent.

I wished it every morning. I prayed for it every night. I did all sorts of weird things to try to make it come true. I tried to walk the entire length of the street without walking on any cracks in the pavement, I counted to fifty without blinking, I kicked every lamppost and muttered, 'Please-please-please.'

Grandad got really worried about me. 'What's up, little Iced Gem?'

'Nothing, Grandad.'

'Don't you nothing me. You're walking funny, you're going all starey-eyed like you're in a trance and you're circling every blooming lamppost like a little dog. There's obviously *something* up.'

'OK, there *is*. But I can't tell you, Grandad. Though I wish I could.'

36

'Couldn't you just whisper it in my ear? I won't be cross or shocked no matter what you've done, sweetheart.'

'I haven't done anything, Grandad. Not this time,' I said, sighing.

'Well, that certainly makes a change,' said Grandad, panting a little as we trudged up and up the stairs to his flat. The lift was broken again and it was a long long haul up to the twelfth floor.

I tried to hop up but I couldn't manage more than three steps. Then I tried running up without stopping but it felt mean leaving Grandad to struggle up all by himself. So then I tried walking up sideways, feet stuck out at an angle.

'We'd better get your mum to take you shopping for new shoes on Saturday,' Grandad wheezed. 'Those ones look too small for you, pet. You're walking all funny in them.'

'I'm just trying to make a wish come true, Grandad,' I said. 'Though it isn't bogging well working.'

'It doesn't sound very nice using words like that.'

'You say it. You say *worse*.'

'Yes, well, I'm a naughty old man. I'm allowed. You're not. Your mum wouldn't like it.'

'I don't care,' I said. 'Grandad, why are mums and dads allowed to boss you about and tell you what to do and where you have to live? Why aren't children counted as *people*?'

'You wait till you get to my age, sweetheart. Old guys like me don't count as people either,' said Grandad. He reached out and squeezed my hand. 'You sure you can't confide in your old grandad, Gem? I won't tell a soul, I swear.'

I couldn't stop myself telling him this time. It just came out in a rush and then I had a little cry. Grandad helped me into his flat, flopped into his big velvety armchair and sat me on his knee. He gave me a big cuddle until I'd stopped crying and then he wiped my eyes with one of his big soft white hankies.

Then he made us both a cup of tea.

'How about a little snack too? I expect you're feeling a bit peckish after all that emotion,' he said.

He gave me a golden syrup sandwich and a slice of strawberry sponge cake and a whole packet of iced gems. Every time I put an iced gem in my mouth I wished that Alice didn't have to go away. I even wished on the little bits of broken icing and the crumbs.

It was all in vain. The next Saturday Alice's mum came round to my house with Alice. Alice was very pale and her eyes were pink, as if she'd been crying a lot. But Auntie Karen was flushed with excitement, starting to talk the minute she was in the front door.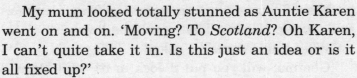

'We've got something to tell you!' she announced. 'We're moving.'

Alice flashed me a warning look so I acted like this was the first I'd heard of it.

My mum looked totally stunned as Auntie Karen went on and on. 'Moving? To *Scotland*? Oh Karen, I can't quite take it in. Is this just an idea or is it all fixed up?'

'It's been in the air for weeks but we wanted to wait to tell everyone until it was definite. Bob's got this brilliant job offer and we're buying this incredible house with an enormous garden. Property's so much cheaper there, though of course Bob will have a hefty raise in salary. It's a perfect place to bring up a family, the countryside's so beautiful. It was such a fantastic chance for us we just couldn't say no. But it'll be a wrench moving all the same. We'll really miss you.'

'And we'll miss you too,' said my mum. She gave Auntie Karen a hug. Then she looked at Alice. 'Oh dear, you and Gemma will miss each other terribly too.'

Alice nodded mournfully, tears dripping down her cheeks.

'Oh Alice, honestly!' said Auntie Karen. 'Come on, you know you're really excited about moving too. You want your pony, don't you, darling? And your own big bedroom with the special window seat and brand new bunk beds—'

'Can I come and stay in one of the bunk beds?' I asked.

'Gemma!' said Mum.

'Yes, of course you can come and stay, Gemma,' said Auntie Karen. 'That would be lovely.'

'*When* can I come?' I asked.

'Gemma, will you put a sock in it!' said Mum.

'Maybe . . . maybe in the summer holidays?' said Auntie Karen.

The summer holidays were months and months away.

I thought how long one *day* felt when I didn't see Alice.

I thought what it would be like at school sitting next to an empty desk.

I thought what it would be like wandering round the playground without anyone to talk to.

I thought what it would be like on Saturdays and Sundays without anyone to come over and play.

I thought what it would be like on my birthday.

I thought of *our* birthday and how we'd made friends when we were tiny newborn babies. And every birthday since, we'd helped each other blow out our birthday candles and make our special wishes . . .

And now those wishes couldn't ever come true.

I looked at Auntie Karen. Her mouth was opening and shutting like a goldfish and all these burbles came bubbling out. She was going to have an Aga in her country kitchen, an ensuite bathroom in the master bedroom, a big barbecue in the patio area, and a garden big enough to stable a pony. Alice could have a real storybook childhood.

I wanted to stopper her mouth and cook her in her Aga and flush her down her ensuite toilet and spear her on her barbecue and trample her to death riding Alice's pony.

Alice herself was slumped in a corner, sniffling. She didn't want to live in a big house with a big garden. She didn't even want a pony, not if it meant she couldn't share it with me.

I took a deep breath, as if I was about to blow out all the candles on my birthday cake all by myself for the first time.

'IT'S ALL YOUR FAULT!' I shouted.

Auntie Karen jumped. Alice gasped. Mum shot up and seized me by the shoulders.

'Be *quiet*, Gemma!'

41

'I *won't* be quiet!' I roared. 'It's not *fair*. I hate you, Auntie Karen. You're taking my best ever friend away from me and you don't even *care*!'

'*Gemma!*' Mum shook me hard, her fingers digging right in. 'Stop that!'

I couldn't stop. I shouted at the top of my voice. Callum and Ayesha came running in from the garden. Dad came downstairs in his dressing gown. Jack came right out of his bedroom and down to the kitchen, Barking Mad yapping hysterically. I yapped higher and every time Mum shook me I screamed at her.

Then Callum picked me right up and hung on tight, even when I tried to hit him. He carried me out of the room and up the stairs and into my bedroom. He sat down on my bed and pulled my dolphin duvet round me, wrapping me up like a little baby in a shawl.

He rocked me backwards and forwards, stroking my scrubbing-brush hair, while I sobbed and sobbed and sobbed. I could feel his arms round me but I felt I was tumbling down down down, past the dolphins on my duvet, right down to the depths of the dark ocean, all on my own.

Four

Alice's mum and dad gave a farewell party to say goodbye to everyone.

'It's a wonder you're invited,' said Mum, glaring at me. 'Screaming like a banshee! I didn't know where to put myself. You try that lark again, young lady, and you'll end up with a good old-fashioned smack-bottom.'

'Now then, love, poor Gemma was upset,' said Dad.

'Well, she'll be even more upset if she doesn't behave impeccably at the party,' said Mum. 'You'll say please and thank you, Gemma, you'll sit quietly and not rush about, you'll keep your voice down, you won't interrupt, you'll eat like a little lady and you'll take care not to spill anything down your dress.'

'What dress?' I mumbled.

'Your party dress, you silly girl,' said Mum.

'I'm not wearing that party dress!' I said.

Mum had spotted this truly terrible custard-yellow frilly frock in last year's sales and she'd

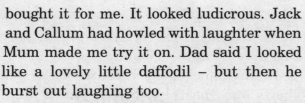

bought it for me. It looked ludicrous. Jack and Callum had howled with laughter when Mum made me try it on. Dad said I looked like a lovely little daffodil – but then he burst out laughing too.

I had torn the dress off and shoved it right at the back of my wardrobe, praying that no one would ever invite me to a party posh enough for me to have to wear the frock.

'This isn't a *party* party,' I protested. 'It's going to be in the garden. Alice isn't wearing a party dress. Oh Mum, please don't make me. I'll look so stupid.'

'You'll do as you're told. It's the perfect occasion. You've got to get some wear out of that dress before it gets too small for you,' said Mum.

I bet she knew all the other kids would be in jeans or shorts. She was just paying me out for being so rude to Auntie Karen.

I knew that if I argued too much Mum wouldn't let me go to the party at all. I had to be a bit artful. I put on my T-shirt and shorts under the Yellow Disaster and decided I'd rip the dress off at the first opportunity.

I still had to wear it *there* though. It looked worse than ever now it was a bit on the small side, cutting me under the arms and showing a lot of my legs.

'Trust you to have ugly great scabs on both

knees,' said Mum, tugging at my hem to try to make the frock longer. 'Do try to stand straight, Gemma. The dress is all bunched up.'

It was bunched up because of the T-shirt and shorts underneath. I stepped out of Mum's reach quickly before she whipped up my skirts and found out. Dad repeated his daffodil remark when he saw me. I expected Callum and Jack to re-run hysterical laughter but maybe I was looking so glum they felt sorry for me. Jack just nodded at me and Callum patted me on the back.

It was weird arriving at Alice's house. It was already looking different, with packing cases in the front room and all the pictures off the wall, leaving ghost imprints on the wallpaper.

I couldn't see Alice among the guests in the garden or the crowd in the kitchen. Alice's mum was looking for her too, calling out, 'Where have you got to, Alice?' She was starting to sound a bit tetchy.

I had a good idea where Alice would be. I peeped inside her bedroom. It looked empty, with packing cases and rubbish bags in a pile in the middle of the room. I opened up Alice's walk-in wardrobe. There she was, sitting cross-legged in the gloom. She was hugging Golden Syrup, her old teddy, rubbing her cheek against his scrubby fur the way she did when she was little.

'Oh Alice,' I said.

I squashed in beside her. We cuddled up close, Golden Syrup squashed between us. Alice's dresses and skirts and jeans tickled the tops of our heads and her shoes and trainers and ballet pumps poked our bottoms.

'I don't want to go,' Alice said helplessly.

'I don't want you to go,' I said.

'It's all got too real,' said Alice. 'I've had to pack nearly all my stuff this morning. It was like it was *our* stuff, Gem, because we've always played together. Mum wants me to throw heaps of things away – my old Barbie dolls, my crayons, my little teddies. Mum says they're just junky old stuff, but they're not, they're special.'

'They *are* junk, Alice. I messed them all up. I gave all your Barbies haircuts and practically scalped them; I scribbled too hard doing the sky and the grass when we drew together so the blue and the green are all broken; and I was the one who gave the little teddies a swimming lesson in your kitchen sink so their fur's been matted ever since. I don't mean to, but I always spoil your things.'

'You don't. Well, you do, but I don't mind it because you invent such fun games. Who am I going to play with in Scotland, Gemma?'

I made Golden Syrup give her a big kiss on the nose. *'You can always play with me, so long as you give me lots of syrup sandwiches,'* I said in a squeaky teddy voice.

'Alice? Alice, where are you?' We heard Auntie Karen open the door. She sighed crossly and then slammed it shut.

'My mum's getting ever so mad,' Alice whispered nervously.

'My mum's *always* mad at me,' I said, picking at the scab on my knee. 'When are you going to let your mum know where you are?'

'I'm not. I don't like her any more.'

'I don't *ever* like my mum.'

'So let's stay here, Gem. I wish we could stay here together for ever and ever.'

'Yeah, they can go off to stupid old Scotland, but you stay living here in your wardrobe. I'll live here too. We'll send Golden Syrup out to forage for food.' I made her teddy bob about eagerly. *'Syrup sandwiches!'* 'he' said. *'Yum yum.'*

'We can't live on syrup sandwiches,' said Alice.

'Yes we can. They're very nutritious,' said Golden Syrup.

Alice pushed him away. 'Gem, I'm serious. Golden Syrup's sandwiches are just pretend. How could we get real food? Could you maybe sneak down to the kitchen and grab a whole load of party food?

47

There's heaps and heaps, Mum was cooking all yesterday. It would last us a couple of days, easy-peasy.'

'You're nuts, Al. We can't really stay in your wardrobe. They'll find us soon, you know they will.'

'Well, let's run away then, before they find us.' Alice seized my hands. 'Let's do it, Gem. Let's really run away.'

'Right. Yes, let's! Only they'll come after us, won't they? Our mums will get in a flap and go to the police and give them our descriptions. *Missing: one girl with long fair hair in pink and one girl with short sticking-up hair in vile yellow frills.* Though I can take it off,' I said, struggling out of the dreadful dress.

'Hey, we'll both change and go in disguise! And I can wear my black pigtail from when I did that Chinese dance at ballet,' Alice said eagerly. 'Pity I don't have two wigs.'

'I don't need a wig,' I said, stepping out of the dress and striking a pose in my shorts and T-shirt. 'I can make out I'm a boy.'

'*Excellent* idea! You can wear my base-ball cap too, that'll make you look even more like a boy. And I'll wear one of my old skirts and tops. Maybe I could rip them up a bit so I look like some really tough street girl.'

48

Alice didn't look at all tough in her shiny black wig and pale-blue skirt and top, even when she'd deliberately cut a big hole in her T-shirt with her sewing scissors.

'Mum will be mad at me when she sees,' she said, poking her finger through the hole.

'Well, she's not going to see, is she?' I said. 'It's just going to be you and me, Al.' I paused, making Golden Syrup jump up. *And me too,* 'he' said.

'Ought we to pack some stuff? Like pyjamas and clean knickers and some washing things?' Alice asked.

Alice's mother came down the landing again, calling her name. It sounded as if she was getting seriously rattled now.

'We haven't got time to pack,' I said. 'Though it would be very useful if you could take some money.'

'Easy-peasy,' said Alice, attacking the underbelly of her china pig. She dislodged the little plastic stopper and he showered her hand with money – several five- and ten-pound notes as well as heaps of coins.

'Oh wow! We're rich!' I said.

We filled our pockets with cash and then listened hard. Alice's mum seemed to have gone downstairs, out of earshot.

'I think the coast is clear,' I said. 'Come on!'

We crawled out of the wardrobe and rushed across the bedroom. Alice had Golden Syrup under her arm. She looked longingly at her bead box and her junior make-up set and my grandma's doll sitting stiffly on her bookshelf.

'Let's take Melissa too,' she said. 'She belongs to both of us.'

'It'll be too much of a bore, lumping her around,' I said. 'And a boy and a tough girl wouldn't be carrying a posh china doll. We look weird enough with Golden Syrup, though he's certainly scruffy.'

Golden Syrup swatted me with his paw. '*Speak for yourself!* You're *the scruffy one,*' 'he' said. '*Look, we could run away to join a circus and I could be your special performing bear. You could both be my trainers. You could wear a top hat and tails like a ringmaster, Gemma, and you could wear a sparkly pink ballet dress, Alice.*' I switched to my own voice. 'Hey, we could have our own circus, right? I can go up on the trapeze and do tightrope walking and tricks on the trampoline, I'd love all that, and *you* can be a bareback rider on a pure white horse.'

'They're called greys.'

'I know, but it sounds silly when you mean white. Hey, maybe it could be a *flying* horse with wings like Pegasus and you could swoop right up to the ceiling of the big top—'

'Big tops don't have ceilings.'

'Alice, will you stop being so picky? We're only *playing.*'

50

'Yes, but this isn't a game. This is real. It *is* real, isn't it? We can really really run away?'

My tummy went tight. I'd thought we were just pretending. I knew just how dangerous it would be if we ran off on our own. I thought how worried Mum and Dad would be even if we were missing just a few hours. Callum would be worried too. And even Jack. Then I thought about Grandad and what it would do to him. He wasn't really all that well. He'd started to wheeze quite a bit when we were out walking. He had to keep having a rest when we went up stairs. What if he had a heart attack with the shock of me going missing?

But Alice gripped my hands tight, her eyes very big and blue and pleading. I couldn't let her down.

'Of course we're really running away,' I said, dropping Golden Syrup on his head to show I wasn't playing any more. 'Come on, then. Let's get going.'

We walked cautiously out of Alice's bedroom, listening hard. We couldn't hear Alice's mum. Perhaps she'd gone to look for her in the garden. We whizzed down the stairs quickly, dodged past some old uncle and out the front door before he'd drawn breath.

We charged down the front path. I vaulted over the front gate just to show off, then I grabbed Alice's hand

and we ran down the road. It felt so weird, the two of us out alone! Even though it was just Alice's ordinary street of neat black and white houses with tidy gardens and clipped privet hedges it felt like we were hacking our way through the jungle, with lions lurking in the shadows and snakes slithering through the creepers.

'It's OK, Alice. We're going to be fine,' I said.

'Let's keep running just in case they're coming after us,' said Alice.

We ran and ran and ran. I'm used to running so it wasn't too hard for me. Alice hates running. By the time we got to the end of the road she was very pink in the face and her black wig was slipping sideways.

'Maybe we should slow down now?' I suggested.

'No! We've – got – to – get – far – away!' Alice gasped.

So we went on running. Alice was bright red by this time and her wig had fallen so far forward she could hardly see where she was going.

We ran past the parade shops. I wondered about asking Alice if we could buy some sweets but it didn't seem the right moment. I tried to ignore the fact that I was starving hungry.

We ran past the park with the tiny toddler swings where we'd dangled day after day when we went to nursery school. Then we ran past our school, all shut up because it was Sunday.

'That's one great thing about running away. We won't have to go to school any more!' I panted.

Alice was so out of breath she couldn't speak at all, but she managed a nod.

We ran down the road with the church with the chiming clock.

'We've been runaways for fifteen whole minutes,' I gasped. I looked round. 'Al, they're not coming after us, honestly. It'll be hours before they twig we're gone. Do let's stop running.'

Alice stopped. She was purple now. The veins were standing out on her forehead. Her eyes were agonized. She leaned against the wall. Her hands clutched her side. She was wheezing worse than Grandad.

'Have you got a stitch? Bend over, that'll make it better,' I said, patting her.

Alice bent over. She looked so weak I was scared she was going to carry on bending until her head went bonk on the pavement. I seized her by the waist, holding her up.

'There! Is that better?' I said, after a few seconds.

'Not – really.'

'Sit down,' I suggested.

I meant on the little wall behind us, but Alice
sat right down on the pavement, without
fussing about dirtying her dress. In fact
she *lay* down,
hands on her
chest, eyes closed.

'Is she all
right?' said a lady
pushing a buggy, gazing at flattened Alice.

'She's fine,' I insisted, although Alice didn't look
the least bit fine. She looked as if she was dead. I
kicked her gently. 'Sit up, Al. Stop messing about.'

Alice struggled upwards. She tried to smile at
the woman to show she was OK, but she still looked
pretty scary.

'Where's your mother, dear?' said the lady.

Alice blinked helplessly.

'She's just in that shop down the road,' I said
quickly. I pulled at Alice's arm. 'Come on, let's go
and find your mum.' I dragged her up and made
her stagger away with me.

'Not – so – quick – I – still – can't – breathe,'
Alice gasped.

'Yeah, I know, but you're making that lady suspicious. We shouldn't attract attention or they'll start
reporting us. We have to wise up.'

'You – weren't – wise – you – said – my – name.'

'No I didn't.'

'You *did*. You said it. Out loud. *Al*, you said.'

'Well, Al could be any old name. It could be short for Alexandra. Or Alicia. Or . . . or Ali Baba.'

'Shut up.'

'OK, maybe we should fix on new names, just to avoid further suspicion. I'm a boy now, so I'll be . . . Michael.' I'm a Liverpool supporter and Michael Owen is the absolute tops.

'OK, Michael,' said Alice, giggling. She'd got her breath back at last. 'So who shall I be? Britney? Kylie? Sabrina?'

'They're all blondes. You're a brunette now,' I said, pulling her wig straight. 'Maybe you should have a Chinese name?'

'I don't know any. Do I *have* to wear a wig? It's so hot and itchy.'

'It's vital. They'll have this message going out on the telly soon, and they'll say you've got long blonde hair and that's the bit that will stick in people's minds. If you've got black plaits and I'm a boy no one will give us a second glance.'

Alice sighed and blew upwards to cool herself, but she didn't protest further.

'You look a bit like Justine in *Tracy Beaker* on the telly,' I said. 'Be Justine. It's a cool name.'

'OK. Justine. Yes, I like it. So will we stay Justine and Michael for good now?'

'You bet. And if we have to go to some new school

I'll stay Michael and then I'll get in all the best football teams and have my own gang. But I'll always play with you at lunch times, Al— *Justine*.'

'Yes, but . . . what school?'

'Well . . .' I gestured vaguely.

'Where are we going to go?'

I thought hard. Where could we go? I thought of all the holidays and days out I'd ever had. I remembered a huge toyshop and a big Ferris wheel and a museum with massive dinosaurs.

'Simple. We'll go to London,' I said. 'Come on, we'll go to the railway station. We've got heaps of money. We'll catch a train.'

Five

We got lost on the way to the railway station. Alice thought it was quite near her granny's church because she'd heard trains rumbling past when she was supposed to be praying. I was pretty sure she was wrong but it didn't seem the right time to have an argument, so we walked all the way to the church.

'What if your granny spots us?' I said.

'Silly, she's back at my house having our barbecue,' said Alice. 'She went to church this morning. I think it's shut up in the afternoon.'

The church wasn't shut up. There were crowds of people chatting and posing for photographs all over the lawn, the ladies flouncing in bright flowery dresses and fancy hats, the men fidgeting in suits and tight shirt collars.

'Is it a wedding?' I asked. Then I saw a plump lady in pink chiffon looking like a very large meringue. She was holding a baby in a white frilly nightie. 'Oh, I get it. A christening!'

57

I'd gone to Alice's christening. Mum had given me an extra big bottle of milk to keep me quiet and I'd thrown up all down the back of her lilac suit. She wasn't pleased. I gave Alice a little Bunnykins mug and bowl and plate. She's still got them, safely stowed away in her mum's china cabinet in their lounge.

Alice came to my christening. I was hungry because Mum hadn't risked feeding me this time. I grizzled throughout the ceremony, and when the vicar started swooshing water at me I shrieked my head off. The vicar had a hard job hanging onto me I was threshing about so furiously. Mum wasn't at *all* pleased.

Alice gave *me* a little Bunnykins mug and bowl and plate. I dropped the mug and broke it the very first time I was big enough to drink out of it. I made mud pies in the bowl and it had to be thrown away. I've still got the plate, but it's got a crack right across it and the edges are chipped.

'Why do I always mess things up, Alice?' I said, sighing.

'I'm *Justine*,' said Alice.

'Sorry!' I said, eyeing the christening party warily in case anyone was listening. 'I'm Michael.'

'Come on, *Michael*,' said Alice, emphasizing my new name.

'Okey-doke, Justine,' I said. I tried to walk with a swagger, like a really cool dude boy.

'Gemma! Alice!' someone shouted.

This very large boy came charging towards us, bellowing our names. I didn't recognize him for a moment because he was squeezed into a small grey suit, all creased and wrinkly. He looked like a baby elephant.

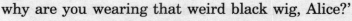

'Oh no,' Alice whispered.

'Oh yes,' I said.

Baby elephant boy was old Biscuits, the boy in our class.

'Why are you walking all funny, Gemma?' he said. 'And why are you wearing that weird black wig, Alice?'

'Shut up, Biscuits! We're in disguise,' I hissed. 'I'm being a boy.'

Biscuits blinked at us. 'Are you a boy too, Alice?'

'No, she's a girl, you nut, she's wearing a dress. But she's got a black plait so she's in disguise too.'

'Shut up, Gem. Don't tell him,' said Alice, pulling at my arm.

She's never thought much of Biscuits. She often got irritated when he and I started to dare each other to do stuff.

'Oh go on. This is dead intriguing,' said Biscuits. 'Tell us what you're up to, Gemma.'

'Tell us what *you're* up to, wearing that daft suit,' I said.

'Yeah, I know. I look a right wally,' said Biscuits. 'My mum made me wear it.' He nodded at the pink meringue lady holding the frilly baby. 'That's my mum. And that's my baby sister Polly. She's just got christened. We're going to have a party at home. There's going to be six kinds of sandwiches, and crisps and sausages and stuff. The christening cake's got thick white icing with POLLY in pink and there's this pink marzipan baby on top. I helped Mum make the cake, and I'm going to get to eat the slice with the baby, she's promised.'

'Yuck!' said Alice. She pulled at me again. 'Come *on*!'

'Come on where?' said Biscuits. 'Where are your mums? Are you out on your own?'

'No,' said Alice. 'My mum's just round the corner.' She's not as good at lying as I am.

'Stuff and rubbish,' said Biscuits. '*What* corner? Hey, you two! You're not running away, are you?'

We both froze.

'Don't be daft!' I said.

'That's me. I am daft. I specialize in it,' said Biscuits, crossing his eyes and lolling his tongue. Then he reassembled his face into a serious expression. 'You *are* running away! You're the daft ones. It's because Alice is moving, isn't it?'

60

'No it's not. Of course we're not running away,' I said, furious that he'd sussed out the situation in seconds. Biscuits was like that. He looked silly and acted silly so much of the time you forgot he had a brilliant brain inside his big head.

'You're bluffing, Gem. I always know when you're bluffing. Remember when you said you weren't feeling a bit sick when we had the weird sandwich competition and you ate my cold Brussels sprout and lumpy custard sandwich? And *then* what happened, eh?'

'Shut up,' I said weakly, my tummy turning over at the memory.

'You mind your own business, Biscuits,' said Alice. 'Come on, Gemma, *now*!'

'Is it just a game?' said Biscuits. 'You wouldn't really be that mad, would you? What are you going to do for food?'

'Trust you to make nosh your number one priority,' I said snippily. 'Don't worry, we've got plenty of cash. Jangle your pockets, Alice.'

'But where are you going to go? Who's going to look after you? What are you going to do if some creepy psycho comes up to you?'

'We're getting the train to London. We'll look after ourselves. And if any creepy psycho comes near us I'll spit in his face and kick him hard,' I said fiercely, and then I let Alice pull me away.

Biscuits called after us, loudly. His mum peered over at us too, *and* some of the christening guests.

'Oh help, we'd better run for it,' I said.

So we ran again. Faster and faster. On and on. Alice went bright pink once more. She kept clutching her side. I knew she had a big stitch in her stomach. So did I. But we couldn't stop or we'd get caught. We struggled on down the road, not daring to look back yet to see if we were being followed. When we turned the corner I spotted a bus that had STATION AVENUE on the front.

'Quick! Jump on, Alice!'

The bus went a very long all-round-the-houses way to the station, but it was good just to flop in our seats and catch our breath.

'I don't know why you had to witter on to that stupid Biscuits,' said Alice. 'I can't stick him.'

'Biscuits is OK. Though didn't he look ridiculous in that suit!'

'He *is* ridiculous. He's so fat,' said Alice, puffing out her cheeks in imitation.

'He can't help that.'

'Of course he can! He goes nosh nosh nosh all day long.'

'Speaking of which, I'm starving! We shouldn't have run away until after the barbecue,' I said, rubbing my rumbly tummy.

'We'll buy a snack when we get off the bus,' said Alice. 'When on earth are we going to get to the station?'

We jumped up and rang the bell as soon as the bus turned into Station Avenue. We were a bit too over-eager. Station Avenue turned out to be a very very long road. Still, we went into a newsagent's and I chose a bar of Galaxy and a giant Mars and a packet of salt and vinegar crisps and a Cornetto ice cream. Alice chose a packet of pink and white marshmallows. I think she picked them because they looked pretty. She only ate a couple – so I helped her out.

'You'll end up as fat as Biscuits if you're not careful,' said Alice.

'You really have a downer on poor Biscuits,' I said, making myself a weird but yummy marshmallow chocolate sandwich. 'Maybe it would be good if I got a bit bigger anyway. I need to look totally different now we're runaways. If I could only grow upwards instead of out I could get some kind of job and then I could earn money for us.'

I'd seen boys working down the market, running and fetching and sorting stuff. I was a good runner and fetcher and sorter.

'I could do it, easy-peasy,' I said, giving Alice's hand a reassuring squeeze.

'You're all sticky,' said Alice, but she squeezed my hand back. 'OK, if you get the job I'll do the shopping and cooking and look after the house. I can cook. Well, I can do toast and boiled eggs and I know how to do stuff out of tins like baked beans.'

'I love baked beans,' I said, but I was thinking about the looking after the house bit. *What* house?

Alice was thinking about it too. 'Where will we live, Gem?' she said in a very small voice. She looked like she might start crying any minute.

'That's simple,' I said firmly. I can never bear it when Alice cries, even though she makes such a habit of it. 'There must be heaps and heaps of empty houses in the whole of London. We'll find one and we'll creep inside. I'll climb through a window – you know I'm good at climbing. We'll clean our house and make it all cosy, our own place, like when we were little and we used to make those cardboard box houses in the garden, remember?'

'Right,' said Alice, though tears were starting to trickle down her face.

We both knew it wasn't right at all. We weren't little five-year-olds playing with plastic tea sets and teddies and Barbies. We were two girls really running away. We didn't have a clue where to go in

London. Biscuits' creepy psycho was starting to stalk me in my head.

'OK, London, here we come,' I said, as we saw the station way down at the very end of the road.

We walked smartly, hand in hand, giving each other brave, encouraging smiles. Alice still had tears dripping down her cheeks but we both pretended not to notice. We went into the station entrance and up to the ticket window.

'We'd like two children's fares to London, please,' I said, dead nonchalantly. I'd been rehearsing what I was going to say in my head for the last five minutes.

'Who are you two kids with, then?' said the ticket man.

I was ready for this too. 'We're with our dad,' I said. 'He's gone to get a newspaper from the kiosk.'

The ticket man eyed me beadily. 'What about his ticket, then?'

'He doesn't need one. He's got a season ticket,' I lied.

Alice looked at me in open admiration. The ticket man certainly seemed convinced.

'Single or return?' he said.

'Single,' said Alice. 'We're not going to return.'

'Fifteen pounds then, dear,' he said.

I felt as if I'd had fifteen punches in the stomach. *'Fifteen pounds?'*

'That's for the two of you,' said the ticket man.

I couldn't believe it was so expensive. Alice scrabbled in her pocket for her money. She found one tightly folded five-pound note. She dug out five gold pound coins. Then another. And another. Two fifty pences. She picked her way through the rest of her change while the ticket man sucked his teeth.

The chocolate and crisps and marshmallows stirred round and round in my tummy like a sourly sweet stew. If I hadn't been so greedy we'd have had more than enough. I felt so ashamed.

'Twenty pence, five pence, one, two, three, four, five, six – and two lots of two pees. Yeah!' said Alice. 'We've got it. Fifteen pounds.'

She piled the change onto the little turntable tray. The ticket man took a long time counting it, checking it twice, but then he printed out our tickets on his machine.

We grabbed them quickly before he could change his mind and darted down the tunnel to the platform. It was a long echoey tunnel so I let out a whoop. It went *whoooop* all around us, as if fifty Gemmas were whooping in a wild chorus.

'Ssh!' Alice hissed. Fifty weeny little shushes reprimanded us.

We both burst out laughing and our giggles echoed above us as we ran the length of the tunnel.

'We've done it!' I said, giving Alice a big hug

when we were up on the platform. The London train was up on the indicator board, due in two minutes. 'We've really done it. London, here we come!'

We hadn't done it at all.

We didn't get to London.

We heard shouting coming from the car park behind the platform. We saw a taxi and my mum and dad and Alice's mum and dad were jumping  out of it. They waved their arms, calling our names.

'Oh help,' I said, clutching Alice. 'Quick! Let's run.'

We had nowhere *to* run. We were trapped on the platform.

I saw the London train approaching in the far distance.

'Oh come *on*, train, *please!*' I willed it to fast-forward so we could leap on board and rush off to our new life in London. But it was still toy-train size and the parents were starting to run up the platform.

Alice's dad caught her up in his arms. Her mum burst into tears. *My* mum got hold of me by the shoulders and shook me until there was a roaring in my ears even louder than the approaching train.

Six

They all thought it was my idea to run away. I decided I didn't care. After all, I didn't want to get Alice into trouble.

I was in BIG BIG BIG trouble. Mum was so mad at me. She managed not to say too much in front of Alice's family but when we got home she shook me again and she shouted, her face so close to mine her spit sprayed in my face. She wanted me to cry and tell her I was sorry. I gritted my teeth and stared straight back at her. I wasn't going to cry one weeny tear. Not in front of her. I *wasn't* sorry. I wished I'd run away for ever and ever and ever.

Mum sent me to my bedroom. I lay on my bed with my face in the pillow. Dad came up after a while and sat down on the bed beside me, patting me awkwardly on the back.

'There now, Gem, don't cry,' he said.

'I'm *not* crying,' I said thickly, my head still in the pillow.

'I know your mum went a bit over the top, pet. But you gave us such a terrible fright. We were so shocked when we got that phone call from Mrs McVitie saying you two were wandering round the town all by yourselves, making your way to the station . . .'

That traitor Biscuits! He'd told on us. Alice was right about him. I wanted to stuff his great gobby mouth with so many of his favourite bogging biscuits – wafers and shortbread and custard creams and jaffa cakes and jammy dodgers and bourbons and digestives and chocolate chip cookies – that he choked to death.

'Didn't you have any idea how dangerous it was to go off like that? Two little girls out on their own . . .' Dad shuddered so that he shook the bed. 'Anything could have happened to you. You must promise never ever ever to try to run away again, do you hear me?'

I didn't want to hear him. I put my hands over my ears. After a while he crept away.

I stayed lying there, head still in the pillow. But then, even with blocked ears, I heard the sound of Dad's taxi starting up. I ran to the window. Mum was sitting in the back looking very boot-faced.

I hammered on the window. 'Are you going back to Alice's house? Let me come too! *Please!* I haven't said goodbye to her.'

Mum and Dad didn't look up at me. The taxi drew off. I went hurtling out of my bedroom, but Callum caught me on the landing.

'Let me go! I've got to go to Alice's,' I shouted.

'You can't go, Gem. You're in disgrace in both houses, you know that. Stop struggling, kiddo. Ouch! Don't kick me, I'm on your side!'

'Then take me to see her! Take me on your bike, Callum, please, please!'

'Look, they won't let you see Alice even if I did take you. Her parents went completely bonkers when they knew you were both missing. You should have heard them.'

'I don't see why. They don't give a stuff about us or they wouldn't separate us,' I said, but I stopped struggling with Callum. 'No one seems to care about Alice and me and what *we* want. Imagine if you weren't allowed to see Ayesha any more.'

'Well, that's different.'

'It's not, it's not!' I said, clenching my fists and pummelling his chest. 'Just because we're kids you think we haven't got *feelings*.'

'OK, OK! Don't get all worked up again. And stop hitting me!' He grabbed my wrists.

I tried aiming a kick at his shin, but I took care just to scuff it with the tip of my trainer. I knew Callum was right. He wasn't much help, but he was on my side.

Jack stayed well clear. He hates any kind of fuss. But Barking Mad came to visit me when I stomped back to my bedroom. He got up on the bed beside me and licked my face lovingly. This wasn't an entirely pleasant experience as Barking Mad is a bit of a whiffy dog no matter how many times Jack tries to bath him and brush his teeth, but he was doing his best to be comforting.

Then I heard Dad's taxi come back.

The front door slammed. Footsteps came upstairs, Mum's high heels going *stab stab stab* on the carpet. She flung open my bedroom door, clutching the crumpled canary dress. She threw it on the bed beside me.

'I hope you're satisfied, young lady! You completely ruined the party. They had to call for a *doctor* because Alice's mum was still hysterical. All the guests have gone home in embarrassment and they've left fifty steaks and fifty half chickens and fifty baked potatoes, all going to waste, *plus* all the puddings, cherry cheese-cake and tiramisu and Mississippi mud pie.'

'Couldn't you have brought some home?' I said.

I wasn't meaning to be cheeky. I was just feeling sad about all that lovely food going to waste – a-little-teardrop sad compared with the enormous Niagara Falls torment of losing Alice for ever. Mum didn't understand.

'You are an *unbelievably* selfish, greedy girl, Gemma Jackson! I can't think how I could ever have had such a daughter. How can you just think of yourself and your own fat little stomach at a time like this?' Mum shouted.

'I *wasn't* thinking of my stomach. Anyway, how can it be fat *and* little? You're not making sense,' I shouted back.

Unwisely.

Mum made me stay in my bedroom and miss tea. I'd already missed lunch, so she was practically starving me to death. OK, I know I had eaten the chocolate and the crisps and Alice's marshmallows but they were just a little snack.

I lay miserably on my bed, my mouth watering at the cooking smells downstairs. Bacon. Lovely sizzling savoury crispy bacon! I put my hands over my rumbly tummy. It didn't feel fat now. I was being starved into a skeleton. Mum would feel sorry when

she came to wake me in the morning and found a
sad little skin-and-bone girl sagging inside her
Incredible Hulk pyjamas.

I tossed and turned, getting all caught up with
the canary satin frock. I batted it away, hating its
slippery floppety feel. I felt something stuck up one
of the big silly puff sleeves. Something rustling and
crackling. A note!

I pulled it out and saw Alice's familiar neat handwriting in her best bright-pink gel ink. The letter
was stiff with stickers, hearts, kisses, flowers, blue-
birds and smiley suns.

Dearest Gem,
I am in disgrace and I bet you are too and
I'm so so so sorry you got the blame. I
tried to tell my mum it was all my idea but
she wouldn't believe me, you know what she's
like. I'm so so so sorry too we didn't get to
say goodbye properly. I wish I didn't have to
go to Scotland. I will miss you so much. I
will NEVER forget you. You are the best
friend in all the world.
Love from Alice. X X X X X ♡

I read my letter again and again, tracing along
each pink line with my finger, stroking every sticker.
Then I hid it between the pages of my best-ever

73

book, *The Enchanted Wood*. It was Grandad's when he was a boy, and when I was little he read it to me. I wished that Alice and I could find the Enchanted Wood, climb up the Faraway Tree, and clamber up the ladder into the land above – and never ever ever come back.

But I was shut up in my bedroom, practically a prisoner. Alice was going to move hundreds of miles away. She'd sent me a wonderful goodbye letter but I had no way of sending her one back. I was so hungry now I couldn't think straight. I went through all the clothes in my wardrobe, searching the pockets of my jackets and jeans. I found a very elderly toffee wrapper in the pocket of my winter duffel coat. I licked it and got a ghostly taste of long-ago toffee which made my mouth water more than ever. I ferreted in my school bag, wondering if I might find a forgotten chocolate bar or a leftover sandwich, but no such luck.

Then I heard footsteps. I hopped back on my bed in case it was Mum. However, the feet jumped and thumped so I guessed it was Callum. He rushed in, shushing me elaborately. He thrust a bacon sandwich in my hand and then leaped out again before I could even thank him properly.

The sandwich was lukewarm and a little fluffy from Callum's pocket but I didn't care a bit. I lay back on my pillows and savoured every bite. Never had a bacon sandwich tasted more delicious. I felt a little guilty having such a healthy appetite on truly the worst day of my life but I couldn't seem to help it. Alice might go off her food entirely but sorrow seemed to make *me* ravenous.

More footsteps. Two steady feet and four scampering paws. Jack and Barking Mad bounded into my room.

'Have you got another bacon sandwich for me?' I asked hopefully.

'Well, I did try to shove one into my pocket for you but Barking Mad wolfed it down while it was still in my hand,' said Jack.

'Oh piffle. So, did you just come upstairs to tell me that?' I said.

'I came to lend you this,' Jack said, handing me his mobile. 'You can text Alice.'

'But she hasn't *got* a mobile.'

'Oh. Right. Well, that idea's not much use then,' said Jack, sighing.

'I could phone her on their land phone.'

Jack peered at me. '*Not* a good idea, Gem. You're not in their good books, to put it mildly.'

'I just want to say goodbye to Alice,' I said, dialling the number.

'Hello?'

My heart sank. It was Alice's mother. I'd hoped

she'd be in her bedroom still having hysterics. I knew I didn't stand a chance now. She'd slam the phone down the minute she heard my voice. *My* voice. I took a deep breath, put my fingers over my mouth to muffle things, and then said in the silliest snobbiest poshest voice ever, 'Oh, good evening, Mrs Barlow. *So* sorry to disturb you.'

Jack stared at me, eyebrows knitted, lips skewed in a question mark. Even Barking Mad stopped panting and looked at me, puzzled.

'Who *is* this?' said Auntie Karen.

'It's Francesca Gilmore-Brown,' I said.

Francesca Gilmore-Brown is a total *pain* of a girl who's in Alice's ballet class. I used to go to ballet too but I got a bit bored and started messing about and the teacher said I'd have to stop going to classes unless I took it seriously. So I stopped because I couldn't *possibly* take that prancing around seriously. I'd hoped Alice would leave too but she actually *liked* ballet, especially as she'd been picked for the end-of-term concert and was all set to wear a sparkly pink tutu and be a Sugar Plum.

Francesca Gilmore-Brown was a Sugar Plum too. She certainly acted in a Sugary Plummy way. She didn't half get on my nerves. She got on Alice's nerves too, but Auntie Karen was dead impressed that a posh rich girl like Francesca wanted to be Alice's friend. She couldn't see that this was never ever going to happen. *I'm* Alice's friend.

'Oh, Francesca!' said Auntie Karen in a silly, simpery sort of way. 'Could you speak up a bit, dear? Your voice is a bit muffled.'

I kept my fingers over my mouth. 'I've just heard that Alice is moving to Scotland. Could I possibly say goodbye to her?'

'Could you say goodbye? Well, Alice is actually up in her bedroom because . . . Well, never mind, dear. Of course you can say goodbye.'

I heard her calling Alice, telling her to come to the phone.

I waited. Then I heard Alice in the background, shouting, 'Is it Gemma?'

'No, it is *not* Gemma. You know perfectly well she's in disgrace. No, Alice, it's Francesca.'

'Who?' said Alice.

'Darling!' Auntie Karen sighed. 'Francesca Gilmore-Brown, the nice little girl from your ballet class.'

'Oh, her,' Alice muttered. 'I don't want to talk to her.'

'Ssh! She'll hear! Don't be so silly, of course you want to talk to Francesca.' I heard a jangle of gold bangle as she handed over the phone. Then Alice was talking to me.

'Hello, Francesca,' she said unenthusiastically.

'It's not silly old Francesca. It's me!' I whispered.

'Oh!' Alice squealed.

'Don't say anything! Don't make your mum suspicious. Oh Al, isn't this awful? I can't believe they're being so mean to us. My mum's shut me up in the bedroom and she's acting like she's going to keep me here for ever and she's not even giving me any food! Can you credit that! She's starving me to *death*.'

'My mum's trying to *make* me eat. We've got all the barbecue food, plates and plates and plates of it, and yet we're moving tomorrow,' said Alice.

'I can't bear it that you're going. If only we'd managed to get that train!'

'I know,' said Alice.

'I wouldn't have cared if we'd had to tramp the streets all night or sleep in the gutter, just so long as we could be together,' I said.

'I think that too,' said Alice.

'Is your mum still hovering?' I asked.

'Yes,' said Alice.

'I wish she'd jolly well bog off,' I said.

Alice burst out laughing. 'So do I!'

'What's Francesca *saying*?' said Auntie Karen.

'She's – she's just telling me a joke to cheer me up, Mum,' said Alice.

'She's such a nice girl,' said Alice's mum. 'Why couldn't you have wanted *her* as your friend?'

'Ssh, Mum,' said Alice.

'If she only knew!' I whispered. 'Alice, thanks so much for your lovely lovely letter. It was brilliant of you to hide it in my horrible frock. Will you write me more letters when you're in Scotland?'

'Of course I will.'

'And I'll write to you too. Heaps and heaps and heaps. And I'll phone too. Every day.'

'Not on my phone, you won't,' said Jack. 'Hurry up, Gem, it's costing me a fortune.'

'I will, Alice. I'll write and I'll phone and I'll come and see you *somehow.*'

'Oh Gemma,' said Alice, sniffling.

Then there was a shriek and a jangle and the phone went dead.

Auntie Karen had cut us off.

It looked like she had cut us off for ever and ever.

Seven

It felt so weird being at school all by myself. Well, obviously, I wasn't literally alone. There were twenty-eight other children in our class and nearly five hundred in the whole school and any number of teachers and classroom assistants and Mr Maggs the caretaker – but it felt like it was one enormous echoing empty building without Alice.

We'd gone to the reception class hand in hand and we'd sat next to each other in every classroom since. I couldn't bear sitting beside Alice's empty chair and desk. I turned my back on it and hunched down small until my chin rested on the table.

Biscuits gave me a poke in the back with a giant Mars bar. 'Hey, Gemma, how come you're suddenly so little? Have you turned into the incredible shrinking girl? You'd better have a nifty nibble on my Mars bar,' he hissed.

I turned round. I stared at him. My eyes burned like lasers. Biscuits looked as if he was singeing.

'What? What's up? What is it? I mean, I know you're probably feeling a bit fed up without Alice. Would you like me to come and sit next to you in Alice's place?'

'No, I wouldn't! I wouldn't want to sit next to you even if you were my best friend because I'd get horribly squashed on account of the fact that you are hugely fat. But as you are now my worst ever enemy I don't even want to be in the same room as you. In the same school, street, town, country, *world* as you.'

Biscuits blinked at me in astonishment, his Mars bar wilting in his hand. 'Don't call me fat! What are you on about, Gemma? We're mates, you and me. We always have been.'

'Not any more, as of yesterday,' I said.

'But I didn't really *do* anything yesterday,' Biscuits protested.

'You told on us,' I said.

'I didn't. Well. I did tell my mum your names when she asked me.'

'Yes, and she phoned up and told *our* mums, as you very well know. And they came swooping off to the station and stopped us running away together. You ruined everything, so you can stop looking all wounded innocence because quite frankly it's a sickening expression and I might just have to punch you straight in your fat chops.'

'I said, don't call me fat! I can't help it if my mum was *concerned* about you. And if you try punching me I'll punch you straight back, so there.'

'Right,' I said. 'OK. We'll fight. At play time.'

'You think I wouldn't hit a girl but I would, if she hit me first.'

'Yeah, and I'll hit you second and third and fourth and I'll go *on* hitting, just you wait and see.' I got so het up I forgot to hiss. I was practically shouting.

'What on earth are you up to, Gemma Jackson?' said our teacher, Mrs Watson. 'Just pipe down, please, and get on with your work. Come along, turn round and leave Biscuits alone.'

'With pleasure!' I muttered, and hunched back in my seat.

Mrs Watson seemed to be keeping a special eye on me. She kept looking in my direction. Towards the end of the lesson she sidled over and peered at what I'd written in my exercise book. I held my breath. We were supposed to write a descriptive paragraph using lots of adjectives. These are describing words. I'd decided to describe Biscuits very graphically indeed. I'd been more than a little bit rude in places. I hurriedly scribbled over the worst part.

'Too late, Gemma, I've already read it,' said Mrs Watson.

I waited for her to hit the roof. But she didn't explode upwards. She sat down beside me in Alice's empty chair.

'It's OK,' she said softly.

I stared at her.

'Well, it's *not* OK to write a lot of abusive rhetoric in your school exercise book, especially about a nice boy like our Biscuits,' Mrs Watson corrected herself.

I didn't have a clue what abusive rhetoric was but it seemed to sum up my Biscuits paragraph pretty neatly.

'Biscuits *isn't* nice,' I mumbled.

'Yes, he is, sweetie. Everyone loves Biscuits, including you. You're not really cross with *him*.'

'Yes I am!'

Mrs Watson leaned towards me and spoke in a whisper. 'Aren't you really feeling miserable because Alice isn't here?'

I struggled to say something. I didn't quite manage it. It felt as if two hands were round my throat, squeezing hard. My eyes were hurting too. I blinked and two tears ran down my cheeks.

'Oh Gemma,' said Mrs Watson. She patted my back gently, like I was a little baby. I *felt* a terrible baby, crying in class. I hunched down even further, so I was practically under my desk.

'I know you must be missing Alice very much,' said Mrs Watson. She gave me one last pat and then went back to her desk.

'Missing' was the most ridiculously inadequate description. I felt as if I'd been torn apart. It was like losing half of me, an eye, an ear, one lip, half a whirly brain, an arm, a leg, a lung, a kidney and half a long long long snake of intestine.

I wondered if Alice felt the same way. At least she wasn't stuck at school next to an empty seat. She was hurtling up the motorway to Scotland. It would be exciting for her, almost like a holiday. And she'd have a new house and new pets and a new school . . . and maybe even a new best friend.

I had no one.

I didn't know what to do at play time. I always went round with Alice, apart from the times Biscuits and I challenged each other to perform amazing feats.

I remembered I'd challenged Biscuits to a proper fight. I clenched my fists. At least it would be something to do. I didn't think Biscuits would be very good at fighting. Not that it really mattered. He could squash me flat for all I cared.

I went looking for Biscuits. I couldn't find him anywhere. I tried the obvious place first, but he wasn't in the tuck shop queue. I trekked the length and breadth of the playground. I searched the corridors, wondering if he might be chomping chocolate in a corner, but there was no sign of him. There was only one place he could be. A place I couldn't go.

I stopped outside the boys' toilets. I waited, arms folded, tapping my toes impatiently. I waited and waited. Boys pushed past me and said stupid things. I made some short sharp comments back to them. I wouldn't be budged, even when they barged into me.

'What you waiting for anyway, Gemma?'

'I'm waiting for Biscuits,' I said.

'Oooh, fancy him, do you?'

'I fancy sticking a skewer in him and roasting him on a spit,' I said. 'Go and tell him I want to get on with our fight.'

'You're wasting your time, Gemma,' said Jack, one of Biscuits' mates. 'He's not in there.'

'I bet he is,' I said.

I had half a mind to march straight in to see for myself, but I had a feeling Mrs Watson wouldn't remain understanding if she caught me fighting in the boys' toilets. I'd be sent to Mr Beaton again. I couldn't go in. I had to winkle Biscuits *out*.

I caught hold of a squinty little kid with glasses dangling skew-whiff off his nose.

'Here, you. Do you know Biscuits? He's that big boy forever stuffing his face who's in my class.'

The kid nodded, trying to hitch his glasses on more securely. Everyone in the whole school knows Biscuits.

'Well, I want you to come back and tell me if he's in the toilets, OK?'

The kid nodded again and backed into the bogs. He was in there a while. He looked shifty when he came out. He was chewing several chocolate toffees, his mouth crammed so full he drooled unattractively. 'He's not there,' he mumbled, slurp running down his chin.

'Oh yes he is. He gave you those toffees as a bribe to say that, didn't he?' I said.

'No he didn't. He gave me the toffees because he said I'm his friend,' the little kid said proudly, and dashed off.

I took a deep breath. 'Right, Biscuits, I know you're in there!' I yelled. 'Come on, come out, you great gutless coward!'

I waited until the bell rang. I waited a minute *after* the bell rang. And then Biscuits' head peered cautiously round the edge of the doorway.

'Got you!' I shouted, and ran at him.

'Help!' Biscuits screamed, and started waddling frantically down the corridor.

'Stop! Come on, you coward, fight me!'

'I don't want to fight! I don't *like* fighting. I'm a pacifist,' Biscuits burbled.

He tried to run away but I lunged forward and caught hold of him by the waistband of his huge trousers.

'Get off!' Biscuits yelled. 'You're pulling them down! You've gone barking mad! First you want to bash me up and now you're trying to take my trousers off. Help! I'm being attacked by a sex maniac!'

'Billy McVitie! Gemma Jackson! What on earth are you playing at?' Mr Beaton bellowed.

Mr Beaton is a horrible headteacher. He's so old and crabby. He's been at our school for centuries. He taught my *dad*, would you believe! Dad said he was just as crabby then, and he used to keep a *cane* in his stationery cupboard. Maybe the cane is still there now.

'Get to your classroom at once!' Mr Beaton commanded. His arm waved in the air, as if he was holding his cane and giving us a good whacking.

I ran for it. Biscuits ran too, though his trousers were halfway down his hips so he had to hobble. He entered the classroom at least two minutes after me, purple in the face and panting.

Mrs Watson had simply shaken her head at me but she told Biscuits off sharply. 'Why are you so exceptionally late, Biscuits? What have you been doing?'

I held my breath. Biscuits was having difficulty *finding* his.

'Sorry – Mrs – Watson,' he wheezed. 'Been – jogging. To – get – fit.'

'Well, it doesn't look as if it's working just yet,' said Mrs Watson. 'And pull your trousers up properly, lad, they look ridiculous.'

Biscuits grinned and adjusted his trousers by wiggling his hips like a hula-hula girl. The class collapsed. I found I was laughing too. Even Mrs Watson had to struggle to stay stern. 'Ever the clown, Biscuits,' she said. 'Still, perhaps we all need cheering up today.'

She glanced at Alice's empty seat. I did too. I wondered why I'd just been laughing when I wanted to cry and cry and cry.

Eight

'Oh dear, what a poor little saddo,' said Grandad when he came to meet me.

He held out his hand. I hung onto it like a little toddler. I didn't want to say anything because I was all choked up. There were heaps of kids from my school milling around us. I didn't want them to see me crying.

I held on until we got to Grandad's block. We swooped upwards in the smelly lift and then we were in the front door and breathing in the safe lovely smell of toast and old books and peppermints.

Grandad sat in his big soft chair and I sat on my big soft grandad. I put my head against his woolly pullover and howled.

'There now, pet,' said Grandad, holding me close. 'That's it. You have a good cry.'

'I'm making your jumper all soggy,' I sobbed.

'No problem. It could do with a good wash,' said Grandad.

He rocked me on his knee while I went on crying. When I reached the snorty trying-to-stop stage he found his big white hankie and let me have a huge blow of my nose.

'I feel such a baby,' I said.

'Nonsense! Everyone needs a good cry. I have a little snuffle myself every now and then,' said Grandad.

'You don't *cry*, Grandad!' I said.

'I do.'

'I've never seen you.'

'I do it in private. The first year your grandma died I reckon I cried myself to sleep most nights.'

'Oh Grandad!' I wound my arms tight round his neck.

I couldn't really remember Grandma. I knew she was small with silver curly hair and little silver glasses, but that was because of the photo on top of Grandad's television.

'Can you remember your grandma?' Grandad asked.

'Yes, of course I can,' I said, because it seemed rude to say no. You can forget some ancient old auntie but not your very own grandma.

'You're a sweet little fibber,' said Grandad, rubbing his nose on the top of my head. 'You were only three when she died.'

'I can so remember her,' I insisted. I racked my brains. I knew Grandma had given me my special doll, Melissa. I wished wished wished I hadn't given her to Alice now.

I thought about dolls. 'Grandma played dolls with me. She made my Barbies dance on one leg, like can-can ladies,' I said.

'That's right, pet!' Grandad said eagerly. 'She had a great sense of humour, your gran. And she loved her dancing. That's where we met, at a dance. Proper ballroom dancing, though we liked to jive around too. We had this special routine where I whizzed her right over my head. Everyone used to clap.'

'I can jive too, Grandad. Callum's shown me.'

'Then what are we waiting for? Let's boogie on down,' said Grandad, snapping his fingers. He tipped me off his lap and got to his feet. He started singing *Blue Suede Shoes* and jogging up and down in his Brown Corduroy Slippers. I jogged around too, waving my arms in the air. Grandad grabbed my hand and twirled me round and round. Then he seized hold of me and tried to whirl me right over his shoulder. He couldn't whirl me high enough and we collapsed in a heap.

'Sorry, sweetheart,' said Grandad. 'I think maybe my jiving days are over now! You'll have to stick to our Callum for a dancing partner.'

'He dances with Ayesha now.'

'Well, yes. That figures. I don't suppose our Jack is much of a lad for dancing?'

'As if!' I said. 'No, *my* dancing partner's always been Alice. Only I'm never ever going to see her again.'

'Yes, you will, darling. You can invite her to come on a visit in the holidays.'

'Her mum wouldn't let her come. She doesn't like me. And I bet she never invites me to stay either. Anyway, how can I ever go all the way to Scotland? The train fare's far too expensive.'

'Well, at least it's a possibility,' said Grandad. He picked himself up and put the kettle on for a cup of tea. 'You *might* be able to make the trip supposing we all saved up or we won the lottery or whatever. Whereas I know I can't ever hop on a train up to heaven to visit your grandma. Well, *one* day that's exactly what I'm going to do, but that's very much single-ticket territory – no chance of a return trip.'

'*Don't*, Grandad,' I said, because I can't stand it when he talks about dying, even if it's just a joke. 'You're not ever ever ever going to die, do you hear me?'

'I'll do my best to stick around for a bit, sweetheart. Now, are you going to join me in a cup of tea?

If you have a ferret in the fridge you might just find a little treat.'

No iced gems today! Grandad had bought *cream cakes*. I opened the box and gazed at them in awe. There was a huge white meringue with a cherry on the top, a glossy chocolate éclair, a scarlet strawberry tart and a large slice of sponge cake oozing jam and cream.

'Oh yummy yummy!'

'Yummy yummy, soon to be in your tummy,' Grandad laughed. 'Go on, then, Gem, you have first pick. But don't tell your mum or we'll both be for it. I know it's naughty but I reckoned my little sweetheart needed cheering up today.'

'I can't choose. I like them all!'

My hand hovered over the meringue, the éclair, the tart, the sponge, circling them several times.

'Take two,' said Grandad. 'Though for Gawd's sake eat your tea when you get home.'

'I will, I will. Oh Grandad, help! *Which* two?'

'I know,' said Grandad, selecting a knife. He cut the éclair neatly in half. Then the strawberry tart, making sure there were two and a half strawberries on each side. Then he severed the sponge into two identical slices. He had most trouble with the meringue. The cream exploded and the meringue collapsed.

'I'm making a right dog's breakfast of this,' said Grandad. 'There, you eat it all up, sweetheart.'

So I ate the whole meringue, glacé cherry and all, and then I ate half the éclair and the strawberry tart and the sponge.

'Oh Grandad, that was the best cake feast ever!' I said.

'My Lord, you must have a tummy the size of a tank,' said Grandad. 'Here, lick your lips. We don't want your mum spotting that cream.'

'No, I don't need Mum to get any madder at me at this present moment in time,' I said, sighing.

But when Mum came to pick me up from Grandad's she didn't have her usual fuss about food. She did tip my chin up and peer at me carefully, but she was looking at my eyes.

'Have you been crying, Gemma?'

'No,' I said firmly.

'Mmm,' said Mum.

Halfway home she reached out and put her arm round me. 'I know you're missing Alice a lot,' she said.

'Oh, well done, Mum,' I said sarcastically, wriggling away from her.

'Now then, madam, don't use that cheeky tone! Look, you're still in total disgrace for all your escapades yesterday.'

'I don't care. I don't care about *anything* any more.'

Mum sighed. 'I know you're feeling very down. Look, Auntie Karen is *my* friend. I'm going to miss her.'

'Not the way I'm going to miss Alice.'

'Yes. All right,' said Mum. 'I know how much Alice means to you. In fact I've often worried about the two of you being so close. Sometimes it's more fun to have a whole bunch of friends.'

'I don't want a bunch. I want Alice.'

'Well, Alice is in Scotland now. They'll be in their new house already, I expect.'

'And I'm stuck here,' I said, as we went up our garden path.

'I know you're feeling miserable just now but I promise you, Gemma, you'll make new friends. You've got *other* friends at school. I was wondering, perhaps you could invite one or two for tea sometime?'

'I don't want anyone to tea.'

'What about that odd boy with the grin? The one who ate up all the trifle at your party? And the ice cream and the chocolate cake and every single sausage on a stick?'

'I *especially* don't want Biscuits.'

'Oh well. I'm only trying to help. You feel sad now but I promise you'll have forgotten all about

95

Alice in a few weeks' time.'

I stared at Mum. There wasn't any point in saying anything at all. It was like we were on totally different planets. She didn't understand at all.

She was doing her best to be kind to me though, even though I was officially in Total Disgrace.

'You didn't end up eating very much yesterday one way or another – through your own fault, of course. But anyway, I thought we could make up for it today. I'll cook your favourite spaghetti bolognese.'

'Oh. Well. Thanks, Mum,' I said.

I remembered the last time I ate spaghetti bolognese. Maybe I didn't really fancy it today. I didn't feel very hungry at all. The two and a half cream cakes in my tummy were taking up rather a lot of room.

'I've got a special pudding too,' said Mum. 'I know how much you love cake. I went to the pâtisserie in my lunch hour and bought a big chocolate cream gâteau.'

I swallowed. 'Mum, the thing is, I'm really not desperately starving hungry,' I said.

'Don't give me that, Gemma. You're always hungry, no matter what.' Mum suddenly frowned. 'Grandad hasn't given you anything to eat, has he?'

'No, nothing, honestly,' I said.

I hoped that by the time Mum had the spag bol

cooked I really would feel hungry. I even ran laps in the garden to work up an appetite. It didn't work. I just felt sick and dizzy.

'What are you up to, sweetheart?' said Dad, coming out the back door. 'I was watching you through the window running round and round the garden. Hey, remember that game I used to play with you when you were tiny? *Round and round the garden, like a teddy bear—*'

'*One step, two step, and a tickly under there,*' I said, tickling under my own chin. 'Only I'm not really ticklish, only under my feet. It's Alice who's terribly ticklish.'

'I'll say! She'd squeal and go all helpless if I even *pretended* to tickle her,' said Dad. He put his arm round me. 'I'm going to miss her too, Gemma. She's been like another daughter to me, bless her. I can't say I'll miss her folks so much. They always seemed a bit stuck up, if you ask me.'

'Especially her mum.' I stuck my chin in the air, patted my imaginary expensive hairdo, and tried out a silly, snooty-pops voice. '*Yes, we're moving to this* fabulous *new house because my Bob's got this* fantastic *job opportunity, and we'll have a brand-new fitted kitchen with an oven here and a hob there, and here a hob, there a hob, everywhere a hob-nob, and we all have our own private bathroom suite with a power shower like Niagara Falls, and our Alice*

97

will have a whole pack *of ponies, and all her posh little riding chums will come and stay with her and she'll like them and make a new best friend—'*

Dad stopped chuckling. 'You're always going to be Alice's best friend, you know that,' he said, ruffling my hair. Then he felt in his pocket and found a Yorkie bar. 'Here. Pop that in your mouth – and don't tell your mum!'

I was feeling a bit queasy. I hoped the chocolate might settle my stomach. I wasn't so sure this was a good idea but I didn't want to hurt Dad's feelings.

It tasted fine at first, just ordinary delicious creamy milk chocolate. Then it got a bit *too* chocolatey. I felt as if I had a mouthful of oozy chocolate mud. I had a hard time swallowing it down.

'Thanks, Dad. That was totally yummy,' I mumbled, my teeth still stuck together. I remembered last Easter when I had five big chocolate Easter eggs and twelve little ones. Biscuits bet me I couldn't eat them all in one go. I insisted I could. I was mistaken.

My tummy started churning unpleasantly at the memory. I decided to go indoors. Perhaps I'd feel a bit better if I had a little flop on my bed.

Callum was just coming in the front door. He had something in his hand, holding it behind his back as he walked past the kitchen door, obviously not wanting Mum to spot it. I nodded wanly at him and trudged upstairs. The smell of the bolognese sauce was making me feel a lot worse.

'Hey, Gem! Hang on a tick.' Callum bounded up the stairs after me. 'How are you feeling, little sis?'

'Not great,' I mumbled.

'Yeah, I thought as much,' Callum said sympathetically. 'Well, this should cheer you up.' He produced a giant whippy ice cream with strawberry sauce and two ninety-nine chocolate flakes.

'Oh!' I gasped.

'Ssh! Don't let Mum hear. You know what she's like about eating before meals. Though I don't know why she fusses so. You never ever lose your appetite.'

'Maybe – maybe just this once – I'm *not* all that hungry, actually,' I said, clutching my tummy. 'Could I maybe eat it later, Callum?'

'But it's starting to drip a bit already. Go on, Gem, eat it up,' said Callum.

So I did. I licked the strawberry sauce, swallowed the ice cream and nibbled my way along both chocolate flakes. I even crunched up the cone. Callum cheered me on all the while.

'That's my little sis,' he said.

I staggered to my bedroom and lay on my bed, clutching my tummy.

At least it was a distraction from the misery of missing Alice. I missed her sooooo much.

The smell of spaghetti bolognese got stronger and stronger and stronger.

'Where are you, Gemma?' Mum called. 'Tea time!'

I sat up very slowly. I took a deep breath. I trailed downstairs. Mum had set the table properly with her best embroidered tablecloth and the rosy plates she usually kept for visitors. The spaghetti bolognese steamed in its special big blue dish. The chocolate gâteau was there too, gleaming on the glass cake plate, oozing cream.

Everyone was sitting up at the table, even Jack. They all smiled at me encouragingly.

'Sit yourself down, dear,' said Mum. 'Right. Let's get you served first.'

She put an extra huge portion of spaghetti bolognese on my plate. I looked at the glistening brown meat sauce and the writhing worms of the spaghetti.

I opened my mouth. And then suddenly I was violently sick – on the spaghetti bolognese, the chocolate gâteau, the rosy plates, the embroidered tablecloth and my own lap.

BLEURGH!

Nine

I was sent to bed in disgrace. It looked like I was going to take up permanent residence in my bedroom. I'd grow white and wasted, stuck in a horizontal position for ever, with only the ceiling to stare at.

I'd be the Girl-in-the-Bedroom, not properly part of the family. Mum and Dad and Callum and Jack would forget all about me. Alice would forget me too. But I'd never ever ever forget her.

I sat up and found my school bag. I inked ALICE IS MY BEST FRIEND FOR EVER all over the cover of my rough book. I wrote it on my book review book and then I opened it up and wrote a review about a book called *Best Friends*. I'd never read a book called *Best Friends*. I didn't know if one even existed. If Mrs Watson queried it I'd tell her I borrowed it from the library.

I'd made up books before. It was more fun reviewing pretendy books than real ones. I once wrote about a book called *One Hundred and One Chocolate Bars*. I described as many as I could, all total invention. Biscuits helped me when I ran out of ideas. His chocolate bars were all giant size with astonishing fillings. I remember his sausage and mash flavour chocolate truffles and his novelty egg and bacon bar. But Biscuits was my Worst Enemy now.

Best Friends

This is the best book ever because of its subject matter, i.e. Best Friends. The girls in this book have been friends all their lives. Then they are separated by their thoughtless selfish families. They end up living hundreds of miles apart. This is HEARTBREAKING I assure you. But the reason this is the best book ever is because it has a happy ending. The girl up in Scotland comes back home because her family hate it up there. They move back to their old house and the two girls are best friends again.

I clasped my book review to my chest, shut my eyes tight, and wished that my story would have that happy ending too.

I heard Barking Mad scuffling on the stairs. Jack put his head round the door.

'How's the Projectile Vomiter?' he said.

'Shut your mouth.'

'No, *you're* the one who should learn to keep her mouth shut. I was the poor sap sitting opposite you. Talk about yuck! And the *smell*! I had to strip off and have a shower, even though I already *had* a shower this morning.'

Jacula Vampire acts like all water is holy and a little sprinkle will make him shrivel up. He's got a cheek moaning about the smell of my sick. It's not always a good idea to get downwind of my brother Jack.

'Just bog off,' I mumbled, burying my head in my pillow.

'Gem? Look, I'm *sorry*.' Jack sat on the end of my bed and took hold of me by the ankle. 'Hey, do you want to ring Alice again on my mobile?'

'I don't know her new number. I need her to phone me. But her mum won't let her. She hates me, you know she does. She wants Alice to forget all about me. And maybe she *will*,' I wailed, starting to cry.

Jack backed rapidly out of my room. He's always fazed if people cry. Maybe it's too watery an experience for him.

He must have told on me to Mum because she came up from the kitchen.

'I've filled the washing machine twice over, and

I've had to tackle the tablecloth by hand. That was a job and a half, I can tell you,' said Mum, wiping her wet hands on her trousers. 'What are you *like*, Gemma? Why can't you be sick neatly down the toilet like everyone else?'

I kept my head in the pillow.

'Are you crying? Jack said you seemed very upset. You're not still feeling poorly, are you? If you're going to be sick again you'd better get into that bathroom pronto.'

'I'm not feeling sick. I'm feeling *sad*,' I sobbed.

Mum sighed. Then she came and sat on the bed beside me. 'Poor old Gemmie,' she said softly.

She used to call me Gemmie long ago when I was little and looked a lot cuter and she still had hopes I'd turn into a curly-girly like Alice.

'I miss her so much, Mum!'

'Oh come on, Gem, you're being a bit of a drama queen now. She's only been gone five minutes. You haven't had time to miss her.'

'But I do! I've seen Alice almost every single day since we were born.'

'I suppose you have. Well, you'll just have to find a new friend now, won't you?'

'I don't *want* a new friend! How many times do

104

I have to say it?'

'Hey hey! Don't take that tone of voice with me,' said Mum, giving me a little shake.

'You don't understand, Mum. Look, what if Dad had to go and live in Scotland. You'd get cross if someone told you to go and find a new husband the minute he was gone!'

'Mmm,' said Mum. She raised her eyebrows. 'Maybe I could be tempted! Your dad's got a bit worn around the edges.' She shook her head when she saw my expression. 'I'm only joking, pet. Of course I wouldn't swap your dad for the world. But losing a friend isn't the same. Look, Karen is *my* friend but I'm not making a big fuss about her going, though I'll miss her a lot.'

Mum wouldn't miss her the way I was missing Alice. Mum and Auntie Karen were never *that* close. They went to keep fit together, and line dancing, and they sometimes went up to London to do a bit of shopping but that was all. They could go *weeks* without seeing each other. Mum had gone off Auntie Karen recently because she'd got a bit snobby and stuck up. Auntie Karen kept showing off about her new blonde highlights and her Juicy sports clothes and her state-of-the-art new mobile . . .

'Mum! Auntie Karen's mobile!'

'What about it?'

'You've got her number! Oh please, let's phone her.'

'Get real, Gemma. She's not going to let you talk to Alice. She says you're a bad influence. Which you *are*, heaven help me.'

'Can't you beg her, Mum? Just for two minutes? I need to know that Alice is OK. I mean, if *I'm* crying just think what she'll be like.'

'Spouting fountains,' said Mum. 'All right. We'll give it a go. If you promise to be as good as gold and stop all this fussing.'

'Right!' I said, bouncing upright.

'Now just take it easy! You've just been sick, remember? *I* certainly do! And don't get all excited because I don't think you'll have much luck.'

We went downstairs to the phone in the hall. Mum dialled the number. She waited. Then she took a deep breath.

'Hi, Karen.' She used her *Can I help you, madam?* shop voice to show she could be dead posh too. 'Yes, it's Liz. So, how was the journey? What were the removal men like? Is it going to be the house of your dreams?'

I knew Mum was simply trying to be friendly and relax Auntie Karen but these questions were fatal. Auntie Karen's voice droned on in Mum's ear for the next ten minutes. Mum murmured politely for a bit but then she started fidgeting. There's no way anyone can interrupt

Auntie Karen when she gets going. Mum raised her eyebrows. Then she held the phone at arm's length. Words like *conservatory* and *ensuite bathroom* and *power shower* buzzed round the room like bees. Mum pulled a face at the phone and mouthed *rabbit rabbit rabbit*. I snorted with laughter and had to cover my mouth with my hands. Mum shook her head at me but she was grinning too.

'It all sounds lovely, Karen, really,' Mum said. 'And Alice is so lucky. Imagine, her own bathroom! How *is* Alice? Our Gemma's very down, missing her so much. Listen, I know Gemma's been a very naughty girl – though actually I don't think that running away idea was *all* down to her. But anyway, do you think you could possibly let her have a little chat with Alice?'

Mum listened.

'She phoned yesterday pretending to be *who*?' Mum said, glaring at me. 'Oh my Lord, what am I going to do with the child? Well, I'll certainly tick her off soundly. Even so, if she apologizes very nicely could she just talk for two minutes to Alice?'

Mum waited.

I waited. I hardly dared breathe. Then Mum smiled and handed me the phone.

'Hi, Gem!'

'Oh Alice, it's so awful!' I said. 'I miss you so much.'

'I know, I know. I miss you too, terribly.'

'Have you been crying?'

'Lots. My eyes are all pink. I cried so much in the car coming up here that Mum got cross with me.'

'My mum's been *very* cross with me,' I said. I glanced at her guiltily. 'But she's being ever so nice now.'

'Well, mine is too, I suppose. And Dad. Golden Syrup got lost in the move along with a whole chest of my things but Dad's bought me a new teddy, a special girl teddy in a ballet dress. She's so cute, with little satin ballet shoes on her paws.'

'What about my grandma's doll?' I asked anxiously. 'She didn't get lost, did she?'

'Oh no, Melissa's fine.'

'Honest?'

'I swear, Gem. Mum wrapped her up in bubble wrap and we carried her in a special bag with all the china ornaments. Mum said I should really have given her back to you. Do you want her back, Gemma?'

I did want her back badly, especially now Grandad had told me more about my grandma, but I didn't like to ask.

'No, I want you to keep her, Alice,' I said. 'When you're feeling extra specially lonely you can give her a cuddle and pretend she's me.'

'I can't *cuddle* her, she'd get spoilt,' said Alice. But then she added, whispering, 'Do you know what I did nearly all the way in the car? I held my own thumb and pretended it was you holding my hand.'

'Oh Alice,' I said, crying again.

'Oh Gem,' said Alice.

I heard Auntie Karen saying stuff in the background, sounding exasperated.

'I've got to go, Gemma,' said Alice.

'Wait! What's your land phone number?'

'We haven't got one yet.'

'Well, what's your address?'

'Greystanes, Rothaven, Angus. I don't know the postcode thingy yet. I'll write, Gemma, I promise. Bye now.'

'We are still best friends, aren't we?'

'You know we are. For ever.'

She switched off the phone. I felt as if I'd been switched off too. I flopped down on the stairs, cradling the phone as if Alice herself was trapped inside.

'Look at you!' said Mum, shaking her head. 'That phone call was meant to cheer you up. Dear oh dear, don't go so dramatic on me. The pair of you are acting like Romeo and Juliet.'

I'd watched the video with Callum and thought it seriously cool, though I couldn't always work out what the words meant.

'I *feel* like Romeo and Juliet. Look what happened to them. They *died*.'

'Yes, well, you've got to go on living, sweetheart. Here, you missed your chance getting your grandma's doll back, you silly girl. Karen had no right to let Alice accept it. And what's all this about you phoning her up and pretending to be someone else?'

'I said I was Francesca Gilmore-Brown. She's this awful snooty-pops girl in Alice's ballet class. I just went, "Oh, I'm *awfully* sorry to bother you, but could I *possibly* have a teensie word with Alice?" and Auntie Karen went all yucky, like, "Oh Francesca, sweetie, how lovely to hear from you. Oh, let me suck up to you because you're so rich and pretty and even posher than us – sooo much more suitable than that scruffy little Gemma who's been such a bad influence on my little angel Alice."'

'You *are* bad,' said Mum, but she was snorting with laughter. 'You've got her voice spot-on, Gemma. You ought to go on the stage.'

I couldn't cheer *me* up but at least I'd made Mum laugh. I put my arms round her neck. 'Thanks for sorting out the phone call, Mum.'

'That's OK. But I can't keep on pestering Karen. You know as well as I do that she doesn't want Alice to stay friends.'

'But ya boo sucks to her, we *are* friends, for ever and ever.'

'Yes, but don't forget Alice will be going to a new school, making new friends.'

'No she won't!'

'You don't want her to be lonely, do you?'

'Well. No. So, OK, maybe she can have one or two just-at-school friends. But I'm still her real best friend.'

'Oh Gemma. I just don't want you to get hurt, love.'

But maybe Alice wasn't going to forget me. She wrote to me straight away, and she put her full address on the back of the envelope.

Dearest Gem,

I miss you so much. It was great to talk to you on the phone. I'd give anything for you to be here with me. I had to go to my new school today and it was so scary. It's an old poky school and we've got an old teacher called Mrs Mackay who's so strict she makes Mr Beaton seem like a cuddly teddy bear.

Hey, did I tell you about Bella, my ballet dancing bear? She is so cute. There's a girl in my form who does ballet and she says I can go to her classes. She's OK and one of the boys said this other boy Jamie thought I was pretty (!!!) but all the others are horrid and they make fun of the way I talk. Only we're not supposed to talk AT ALL in class or Mrs Mackay gets mad. You would be in so much trouble if you went to my new school, Gem.

I haven't got started telling you stuff about the new house and my new bedroom (it's pink and I wish you could see it) but my hand is really aching with all this writing. I wish I had a computer.

I miss you.

Lots and lots of love from your very best friend

Alice X X

Dear Alice,

Thank you soooooooo much for your letter, but can you write an even longer one next time, please please please? If your right hand gets tired try using your left hand instead. I don't mind a bit if your writing is wobbly. Or you could try holding the pen in your teeth or whip your shoes and socks off and write with your toes. But I need you to tell me how you are and whether you've been crying and if you're having bad dreams and I want to know exactly how much you're missing me. Ok,

here's a little questionnaire for you!
Do you miss Gemma:
a) Not at all, in fact you're not even sure who Gemma is, though her name sounds vaguely familiar?
b) Occasionally, when you glance at Melissa?
c) A lot, and you sometimes sigh sadly and whisper, 'Oh Gem, I wish you were here'?
d) desperately - you think about her all the time and wish wish wish you were back being her best friend where you belong?
I don't miss you a) or b) or c) or even d) - I go way down the alphabet to z). I have been crying and crying and crying. My eyes are as crimson as blood and Mum keeps having to get her bucket and squeezy mop to soak up my pool of tears. Hey, she had to get out all the cleaning stuff in her cupboard the other day because I was sick all over everywhere because I was in such a traumatized state. I'd also eaten rather a lot of cakes and chocolates and ice cream. Grief doesn't make me lose my appetite. It makes me hungrier and hungrier. Beware! When we eventually get

113

to see each other again (when??? how????) you
probably won't recognize me. I shall be as fat
as horrible hateful stupid old Biscuits.
Fatter! Imagine. We won't be able to cuddle
up in bed if we have a sleepover because I
might roll over on you and squash you flat.
Still, if I can grow as big as a house then
Mum and Dad won't be able to tell
me what to do. I'll tell them!
I'll say, 'Right, give me lots of
money,' and then I'll hire a giant
helicopter and wedge myself into it
somehow and I'll whirr up to
Scotland in a matter of minutes and
snatch you up and then we'll go off adven-
turing together and if your mum and dad try
to stop us I'll stamp on them, Ok?
Lots and lots and lots and lots of love from
your all-time best friend
Gemma   X X

Dear Gem,
I'm writing this at school because my mum
says she doesn't want me to write to you
any more. You'll never guess what she did.
She opened your letter to me and she didn't
like it one bit, especially the part where you
said you'd stamp on her. And she fussed

about the helicopter stuff too. Like you could <u>really</u> hire a helicopter! But anyway, she says I mustn't write back and we've got to stop being friends, but don't worry, <u>of course</u> we'll stay friends - and listen, Gem, I've got a brilliant way of us writing to each other!!! There's this girl in my class, Flora - you know, she does ballet too. Well, she saw I'd been crying and asked why and so I told her I was missing you and my mum won't let me write etc. etc. etc. and she said why didn't I e-mail and I said I haven't got my own computer and I'm only allowed to use my dad's if he's supervising me and she said she's got a computer and I can go round to her house and send you an e-mail any time I want. I know you haven't got your own computer yet but what about your brother Jack??? Flora's e-mail address is floraweegirl@hotmail.com. I do do do hope we can e-mail each other, Gem!

Did I tell you about my new bedroom? It's amazing. Flora says she thinks it's the most beautiful bedroom she's ever seen.
Your best friend for ever,

Alice   X X X

Ten

'Give us a hand with the dishes, Gemma,' said Mum, piling them up in the sink.

'Oh Mum! That's not fair. The boys never help,' I said.

Callum and Jack slipped smartly upstairs.

'Jack, wait for me!' I called.

'Why are you always hanging round Jack nowadays?' Mum asked suspiciously. 'You keep disappearing into his room.'

'He's just letting me use his computer for a bit, Mum,' I said. 'He shows me how to look up stuff on the internet.'

'Hmm,' said Mum. She still looked suspicious. 'What *sort* of stuff? It's nothing naughty, is it?'

'Mum! No. No, it's for this project thingy.'

'What project? Is it for homework?'

'That's right. Homework,' I said quickly.

'You've never been bothered about making an effort with your homework before,' said Mum.

'Are you telling the kid off for trying hard with

116

her homework?' Dad called from the sofa in the living room. 'Give her a break, Liz.'

'Yeah, Mum, give me a break,' I said, dodging out the way as she swatted me with the tea towel.

I was determined not to get lumbered with any more chores like the boring old dishes. I was working flat out as it was, appeasing Jack. He let me use his computer to e-mail Alice via this Flora girl and he saved her e-mails back to me – but at a price. He didn't demand actual cash as he knew I didn't *have* any. No, I had to act like his general servant, finding all his pongy old socks from under his bed and putting them in the laundry basket, dusting the geeky collection of paper aeroplanes dangling from his ceiling, even rinsing round the bath after he'd used it.

'Would you like me to flush the flipping toilet for you while I'm at it?' I added sarcastically.

This was a big mistake.

I also had to change his horrible dinosaur duvet cover, a job I hate hate hate. I was far too exhausted afterwards to tackle changing my own duvet and Mum lectured me for hours.

'I was just too tired to change it, Mum,' I said truthfully.

Mum went on and on about how tired *she* was, running the house for a family of five. Surely it was the least a daughter could do to lend a hand? Even Jack was getting a lot more responsible now about his laundry and keeping his room spick and span even though he was so busy with all his school studies, *plus* being the number one dog walker in the family.

I wouldn't have minded walking Barking Mad myself as one of my chores but Jack wouldn't let me. However, if he let Barking Mad off the lead up the common he would roll in the smelliest dungheap he could find. Barking Mad, that is, not my brother. Then guess who had to try to give the silly dog a bath. Me!

But all these extra chores were worth it as I could now communicate properly with Alice. I didn't like having to start off tapping out a message to Flora first. I didn't much like the sound of her.

Still, I tried to be ultra polite as she let Alice use her computer.

 Hello, Flora. It's me, Gemma, Alice's best friend. Thank you very very very much for letting us write to each other. Now, here is my private message for Alice. Don't read it, OK?

Dearest Alice – How are you? Are you still missing me LOTS and LOTS and LOTS? I am missing you MORE if that is possible! It is so lonely and no one understands and they're all being hateful to me.

Oh! Jack has just looked at the screen and he says *he's* being exceptionally kind to me by letting me use his computer. I suppose that's true, but it's at GREAT COST to me!

Callum is being OK too actually. He took me out to McDonald's yesterday evening and he bought me a Happy Meal and when it didn't have the special Blue Two Kung Fu Fighter toy I particularly wanted he bought me *another* Happy Meal and the little blue guy was in that, so now he's got Red Zed to fight with. Yay! I expect Callum only asked me out because Ayesha was seeing her girl-friends, but it was still sweet of him.

Grandad's being so kind too, though he won't buy me cream cakes any more. Dad keeps tickling me to try to make me smile. Mum *was* OK for a bit, but now she's nag nag nag as always.

Still, they're mostly all right at home – but it's HORRIBLE at school. Mrs Watson *was* quite nice for a bit but now you will never ever ever guess what she's done! We have to do this stupid project about a famous person with a partner and she says I have to be partners with *Biscuits*! I am not not not going to be his partner. Do you have to be partners with anyone at your new school or are you allowed to work on your own if you want?

Lots and lots and lots of love

From your best ever friend for always

Gemma

Hi Gem! Thanks for your really really really long message. I can't write back as much because it would be a bit rude to Flora seeing as it's her computer. I've got to be quick anyway because we've got a ballet class at five. Flora's mum is taking us. I do hope I do OK. Flora is BRILLIANT at ballet, heaps better than me. I hope I'm not the worst in the whole class.

What's this project? Poor you getting stuck with Biscuits. They're in the middle of this Egyptian project in my new class and I got worried because I didn't know anything about them but Flora's lent me her notes, so she's sort of my partner, I suppose. It's very kind of her to help me out.

This is not just a pretty pattern. It's an Egyptian hiero-glyphic.

Lots and lots of love

From your best friend

Alice

Hello, Flora. This is a very private message for Alice. You stop reading now.

Dearest Alice – You know HEAPS about the Egyptians. Don't you remember, Callum took us up to London and we saw the mummies in the museum and it was so cool – only you found it a little bit creepy, even the cat mummies. But I bet the computer girl Flora hasn't seen real mummies. You tell her all about them. And I'll make you up a story about them. I'll get to work on it right away, all about a Terrible Curse and a mummy who comes back to life and its bandages fall off and little blackened bits of flesh crumble off too. It will be dead scary and will seriously impress all your new classmates. Only don't get too matey with anyone in particular, will you?

Lots and lots and lots of love

From your best ever friend who will never ever break friends

Gemma

I was *certainly* not matey with anyone at school. Especially not Biscuits. I wasn't speaking to him, which made this stupid project a bit of a problem. Still, I thought I'd solved things. I didn't speak *to* Biscuits; I addressed the space in front of him, and announced my intentions.

'I'm doing my Famous Person project on Michael Owen because he is the best footballer ever and you can't really get more famous than that. I've got all this stuff about him and I can just copy it out easy-peasy and cut out a few photos from the papers and I *might* even include one of my posters for the project presentation.'

I thought I was being ultra kind and generous saving Biscuits an immense amount of work. Was he grateful for my suggestion? Absolutely *not*!

'I think you've got something wrong with your eyes, Gemma. You're talking to me but you're staring into space. It's very spooky.'

'I'm *not* talking to you, Biscuits. I told you, I can't stick you. If you weren't such a rotten coward I'd fight you. I'm simply speaking out loud. Talking to myself about this project.'

'Talking to yourself is the first sign of madness,' said Biscuits. 'I'm not surprised. I think you've gone seriously bonkers, Gemma Jackson. Still, you're supposed to humour lunatics, so I will. Only I'm *not* doing a project on Michael Owen. I'm not into football. I don't know anything about him.'

122

'You don't *need* to know. I'm telling you, I've got all this stuff.'

'But I want to do something different. Heaps of people are doing footballers, your Michael Owen or David Beckham. I want an *original* choice.'

'Oh yeah, like who?'

'Fat Larry.'

'Who?'

'You've never heard of *Fat Larry*?'

'Are they like a pop group?'

'It's a him. Larry. Who's fat. He's this brilliant TV chef – you *must* have seen him. He wears these amazing huge sparkly suits and a big diamond earring.'

'Oh, very tasteful – *not*.'

'And each programme he cooks for a different group of people, like kids in hospital or old ladies in a home or a group of mums on an estate. They always look sad or weird or bored to start with, and not really into food at all, but Fat Larry cheers them all up and cooks them something yummy and at the end of the programme they're all laughing and eating and having a whale of a time. And there's a cartoon of Fat Larry as a whale at the end of the programme after the credits.'

'What are you, a publicity guy for this Fat Larry?'

'I just think he's great, that's all. He's famous. I want to do a project on him. I bet nobody else is.'

'Yeah, because nobody else *cares* about Fat Larry. Look, we're doing a Michael Owen project. I *said*, I've got all the info—'

'And so have I. I've got all three Fat Larry cookery books.'

'Oh, big deal.'

'With recipes. We could make stuff for when we present our project.'

I looked at him properly. 'What sort of stuff?'

'Anything! We could have little trays and pass canapés around – or little cakes – or mini pizzas. Whatever. I could do a cookery demonstration Fat Larry style. I know heaps of his jokes. And I kind of look like a little Fat Larry myself. Hey, maybe my mum could get some sparkly material cheap down the market and make me my own miniature Fat Larry suit!'

'*I* could do football demonstrations. I've got a Liverpool football kit so I could be Michael Owen,' I said, but my voice lacked conviction. I was only arguing for the sake of it. I could see Biscuits' project was a brilliant idea. For *him*.

'Suppose you did do Fat Larry? What could *I* do?'

'You could read out the recipes,' said Biscuits.

'What, like your assistant? No way. *I'll* be Fat Larry and *you* can read out the recipes.'

'You're just being daft now. You don't look anything like him.'

124

'I could impersonate him, easy-peasy.'

'But you've never even seen him on the telly! You're being dead awkward, Gem. Still, I'll make allowances seeing as you're going through a sad time missing Alice.'

'All because of *you*.'

'No it wasn't. And you know it.'

I suppose deep deep deep down I knew it wasn't really Biscuits' fault. Alice and I would have been caught whether he'd told on us or not. Or we'd have got the train back home again anyway because I knew we couldn't *really* live in London all by ourselves. But I didn't feel ready to acknowledge any of this, particularly to Biscuits.

'It *was* your fault, Fatso.'

'Fatso *Larry*! *I'm* going to be him, do you hear?'

'No, *I'm* going to be him and I'll get my mum to make *me* a sparkly suit, see. Now clear off. I'm not speaking to you, remember?'

'For a girl who's not speaking you don't half gab gab gab,' said Biscuits cheerfully. He produced a large tinfoil package from his school bag and unwrapped it carefully. It was two slices of the most fabulous mouth-watering chocolate cake decorated with scarlet cherries and white whipped cream.

Biscuits took a very large bite. Cream and chocolate oozed all over his fat fingers.

He licked them happily, one by one. 'Yummy,' he said. 'A special Fat Larry recipe. Delicious! Though I shouldn't say that, because I made it myself.'

'You can't make cake like that, Biscuits!'

'I can so. Well, my mum helped a bit.'

'You mean *you* helped *her*.'

'You can scoff all you like, Gemma, but when I'm presenting our Fat Larry project you'll *see* I can cook.'

'When *I'm* being Fat Larry you'll see *I* can cook,' I said, although my heart was starting to beat faster.

I was pretty sure I could pretend to be Fat Larry easily enough once I'd sussed out what he actually looked like, though I wasn't totally sure I could get Mum to make me a suit, sparkly or otherwise. But actual cookery was something else altogether.

I'd once tried to make pancakes for Alice and me when Mum was working late and Dad was asleep. I'd watched Mum on Pancake Day and it looked dead easy. Alice wasn't so sure. She was right.

I whipped up some eggs and some milk and tipped some flour in but it all went lumpy. I hoped it  would all blend together in the frying pan. It didn't. I turned the heat up to encourage it. Then I chatted to Alice and ate a few raisins and dug my finger into the butter and coated it with sugar as I was getting ravenous by this time. Then I noticed a funny smell. When I investigated I found the lumpy pancake was rapidly turning black. I thought it might help to toss it. *Big* mistake. Crispy cinders flew everywhere and fat spilled all over the stove.

We tried to clean it all up but we couldn't quite manage it. The frying pan was coated in a thick black crust and we couldn't shift it.

I don't want to remember what happened when Mum came home. It's too painful. I've never wanted to try my hand at cooking again – put it that way.

'Tell you what. Let me be Fat Larry and I'll give you half my cake,' said Biscuits, holding a slice right under my nose so I could smell its divine rich chocolate.

I so wanted a slice.

I didn't want to cook. I didn't really want a sparkly suit. I didn't even want to track Fat Larry down on the telly. But I couldn't give up now. I didn't want to give in to Biscuits.

I didn't want to make friends.

'Yuck,' I said. 'I absolutely hate chocolate cake. And *I'm* going to be Fat Larry, so there!'

Eleven

'Have you ever heard of Fat Larry, Grandad?' I asked, as we walked home from school.

'Yes, he's a TV chef, a bit of a laugh. I don't mind his programme, but Nigella's *my* favourite.' Grandad started burbling on about this Nigella until I tugged at his sleeve.

'No, Grandad, I need to know about Fat Larry. When's he on the telly? I want to watch. Why haven't I ever seen him?'

'He's on at half past seven. Your mum will be watching her *Corrie* then, won't she? I'll video Fat Larry if you like, pet.'

'Can you do the Fat Larry recipes, Grandad?'

'You're joking, aren't you? I'm not one of these new men. I'm an old man and my limit's blooming beans on toast, you know that.' Grandad sighed. 'I'd give anything for one of your grandma's roast beef dinners with lovely golden Yorkshire pudding! And she used to make wonderful trifle – and apple pies – and fruit cake . . .'

'Maybe I'll take after her. I'll make you lots of lovely nosh, Grandad.'

'You're a very talented girl, little Gem, but I don't think you're a natural cook. Your mum told me all about the dreaded pancake disaster.'

'She stopped my pocket money for *weeks* to pay for a new frying pan. She hardly uses it now anyway because she says fried food is bad for you. Grandad, Mum doesn't make Yorkshire pud but she does do roast chicken on Sundays sometimes. Why don't you come round for lunch?'

'That's sweet of you, Gemma. But I'm generally quite happy pottering down to the pub of a lunch time – or I'm out working at weekends, when they're short of a driver. Maybe I can wangle you another little trip in the white Rolls if I'm booked for a wedding, sweetheart. What are you up to on Saturday?'

'Nothing,' I said, sighing.

I didn't know what to do with myself. I plagued Jack until he let me send a long e-mail to Alice. I'd wondered if she might be playing round at Flora's house, so I could get a reply straight away. No such luck. I badly wanted to hear from her but it was actually a relief to know they weren't weekend friends. I didn't like the sound of this Flora one little bit. It looked like she was trying to get Alice to be *her* best friend. Still, she didn't stand a chance. I knew that.

Callum asked if I wanted to go for a walk down the park. He took his bike and let me muck around on it, trying to do all sorts of daft tricks. They didn't always work. The third time I fell off I scraped a teeny bit of the paintwork. I held my breath because Callum's ultra picky about keeping his bike pristine, but he barely looked at it. He fussed about my knees instead, spitting on a scrubby bit of tissue, trying to get them cleaned up.

'Ouch!' I said. 'Sorry I scratched your bike, Cal.'

'That's OK.'

'I'm rubbish at riding it.'

'No you're not. You'd be great, it's just your legs are still little and my bike's way too big. We're going to have to get you your own bike, Gem.'

'Oh yeah,' I said, because bikes cost a fortune.

'We could look for a little second-hand one, something that maybe needs fixing up a bit. I could do that for you! It could be your birthday present.'

I thought about my birthday next month. The first birthday without Alice. 'I don't think I want to bother about my birthday,' I said.

'That's daft, Gem. We'll make it a really special day, you'll see,' said Callum.

He was trying so hard to be sweet to me (even though he was hurting my knees horribly) but I couldn't pretend.

'It can't be a special day without Alice,' I said, and I burst into tears.

Once I'd started I couldn't stop. Callum didn't have any more tissues to mop me with so he popped me on the saddle and wheeled me home quick.

Mum was out working so she couldn't tell me off about my knees.

'We'd better wash them properly and put some sort of stuff on them to stop them going mouldy,' said Callum. 'Where's Dad?'

He wasn't lying on the sofa watching television. He wasn't still in bed. The taxi was parked in the driveway so he wasn't out at work.

'So where's he got to?' said Callum, taking me by the hand. 'Maybe he's in the garden?'

Mum had been having a right old nag at him recently to mow the lawn, but the grass was still ankle-high and spattered with gold dandelions. There was no lawn-mower noise but we could hear a distant sawing.

'Dad?' Callum called.

There was a muffled shout from the old shed at

131

the bottom of the garden.

'Dad, what are you up to?' Callum yelled, taking me down the garden. 'Look, Gemma's hurt herself.'

'She's what?' Dad shouted, still sawing.

Callum opened the shed door. 'Look at her knees,' he said.

But Dad immediately shoved the door shut again. 'Dad?'

'Just a tick,' Dad called.

We could hear him bustling around. Then he opened the door to us. There was an old tarpaulin thrown over his workbench.

'What's under that?' I sniffled.

'Never you mind!' said Dad. 'Oh Gawd, look at the state of you! What are we going to do with you, Gem? You're always in the wars.'

I felt like I really had been in a war. And I hadn't won. I was totally defeated.

I didn't want to do anything. I sprawled on Dad's sofa most of the time, watching television. I didn't always watch the screen.

I stared into space and saw Alice instead.

Sometimes this phantom Alice waved to me and told me how much she was missing me.

132

She sometimes cried too. But other times she was smiling. She wasn't smiling at me. She was smiling at this Flora girl. Then they'd both wave at me and scoot off together, arms linked.

Mum came home from work and caught me crying. She thought it was my sore knees. She went on and on about them. 'The last lot of scabs have only just cleared up, you silly girl. What am I going to do with you, eh? How can we get you all dressed up nicely in a pretty dress if you've always got cuts and scrapes and bruises all over you?' she said, dabbing Savlon on my knees.

'Ow! I don't *want* to get dressed up nicely. I hate getting dressed up. I especially hate dresses.'

'Yes, well, that lovely yellow dress will never be the same again,' said Mum, shaking her head at me. 'You were such a *naughty* girl, Gemma. What a waste of money that dress was! I thought you could wear it for your birthday party—'

'I don't want a birthday party this year,' I said. 'Not without Alice.'

'Of course you do. You can invite some of your other friends,' said Mum.

'I haven't got any other friends,' I said.

'Don't be so silly, you've got heaps of friends, dear. What about that funny boy with the silly nickname. Cookie? Chocolate? Pudding?'

'I haven't got a clue who you're talking about, Mum,' I lied.

'Well anyway, you start thinking about who you want to invite.'

I put my chin on my chest. 'Alice,' I mumbled.

Mum sighed. 'There must be *some* girls in your class that you like, Gemma.'

'They're all right, I suppose. But they're just not my *friends*.'

'Maybe a special birthday party would be an excellent way of *making* friends. So what are you going to wear, hmm? I realize you don't like yellow. What colour dress *would* you like?'

I shrugged my shoulders. I thought about the message Alice had tucked into the sleeve of the awful canary dress. Tears dribbled down my cheeks.

'Now stop that silly crying,' said Mum, but she sat down on the sofa beside me and put her arm round me. 'What about blue for a dress? You like blue, Gemma.'

She had another look at my shredded knees. 'Maybe I'm wasting my time talking about dresses. Suppose we bought you a smart little pair of trousers, really well cut, with a designer T-shirt? Would you like that, poppet?'

'I know what I'd really really like as a party outfit,' I said suddenly. 'I'd like a great big sparkly suit.'

Mum gave me a double-take. 'A great big sparkly suit?' she said wearily. 'Don't be silly, Gemma.'

I decided not to push too hard just yet. I'd have to work on it. Besides, I wasn't quite sure exactly the kind I wanted.

Grandad remembered to video Fat Larry and showed me after school the following week.

'It's quite a good show. That Fat Larry's a right laugh,' said Grandad. 'He's certainly a good advert for his nosh. Look at the size of him!'

Fat Larry was very very fat. His crimson sparkly suit was very very big. I'd have to stick a cushion down my trousers to pad myself out a bit. *If* Mum made me the trousers. She kept telling me there was no way her little girl was going to wear such a bizarre outfit at her own party. I hoped she might weaken.

I watched Fat Larry very carefully indeed. When the programme finished I asked Grandad if we could watch it again.

'Again?' said Grandad. 'You're a funny girl, our Gem. Have you got a little crush on this Fat Larry? You were staring at him like you were transfixed. Don't tell me you've fallen in love!' Grandad wiggled his eyebrows and made kissing noises.

'I don't *love* Fat Larry. I just want to look like him,' I said.

Grandad's eyes popped. 'You're one weird little kid, sweetheart,' he said, but he replayed the video for me.

I watched Fat Larry bouncing round the studio as if he had springs in his chunky suede shoes. I watched Fat Larry wave his big arms like windmills. I watched Fat Larry shaking seasoning into his stewpan as if he was playing the maracas. I watched Fat Larry taste his chocolate cake and lick his lips s-l-o-w-l-y like the happiest cat in a vat of cream.

When Grandad went out the room to make a cup of tea I tried a bounce, a wave, a shake, a smile. I felt a little tingle up and down my spine. I was getting it.

I made Grandad promise to video Fat Larry every time he came on television.

'I'm sure you can buy videos of his old shows,' said Grandad. 'If you're *really* into this fat old guy I could give you a couple for your birthday.'

'Oh Grandad, don't you go on about my bogging birthday too,' I said. 'Everyone keeps asking me what I want. I know they're only being kind but I don't really want anything, apart from a Fat Larry suit.'

'Oh my Gawd,' said Grandad. 'What's your mum going to say about that, eh?'

'She's going to make me one,' I said.

'Oh yes?' said Grandad.

'Well, she might. Grandad, you can sew, can't you?'

'I'm a dab hand at button sewing, darling, but I could no more make you a sparkly suit than fly to the moon.'

'I don't want to fly to the moon, Grandad. Just Scotland. I got Jack to look up the air fare on the internet, but it costs over a hundred pounds so I haven't got a hope in bogging hell.'

'Tut! Language. Look, maybe you'll get to go up to Scotland for your holidays sometime.'

'No I won't. Dad says he just wants to lie on a beach in the sun. He says Scotland's too cold. And Mum wants to go somewhere where there's lots of shops and Alice's house is right out in the country and they haven't *got* any shops. And it'll be too *late* in the summer holidays. I need to see Alice now, on our birthday.'

I started crying. Grandad pulled me onto his lap. I leaned my head on his old jumper and breathed in the warm woolly smell.

'What's getting you all worked up about this birthday, pet?' Grandad asked.

'We always make a birthday wish, Alice and me,

137

that we'll be best friends for ever and ever. Now this birthday we won't be together and I'm dead scared because Alice has got this new friend, Flora. She goes on and on about her in her e-mails. What if Alice asks Flora round for tea on her birthday and they cut her birthday cake together and Alice and Flora make the best friends wish?'

I'd been thinking this for days and days but the words just wriggled in my brain like little maggots. Now I'd said them out loud they seemed to be buzzing round the room like angry wasps, stinging and stinging.

Twelve

Grandad said Flora couldn't possibly be a patch on me. He said Alice had only known Flora five minutes and she'd known me all her life. He said Alice and I were closer than sisters and even if we weren't together we were always going to be there for each other, best friends for always. He said that he and Grandma had always been best friends and they'd stayed that way even when he had a job out in Saudi which meant they were parted for months at a time. He said all this and I listened.

I still worried.

I went on and on worrying. I sent Alice long e-mails every day. I *hated* having to do this via Flora. What a stupid name! I started calling her Margarine Girl in my head. I was so sick of hearing about her brilliance at bogging ballet and her beautiful bedroom and her lovely cool clothes. They sounded rubbish to me, silly tops showing her tummy and tight little skirts and shoes with real heels. I like to keep my tummy well hidden and I hate tight skirts because you can't run and heels are stupid because they catch on things and make you walk all wobbly with your bum sticking out.

I think I maybe said some of this in one of my e-mails. Alice's mum wouldn't let *her* wear crop tops and tight skirts and shoes with heels because she said Alice was still a little girl so why dress like she was going to a nightclub? Alice had always agreed with me that these clothes were stupid anyway but now she e-mailed back: 'You are soooo hopeless, Gemma.' She then wrote heaps about Flora's new kitten heels and how they were the exact same shoe size so Flora let her borrow them, because 'she's soooo kind'.

I had Flora sussed out. She wasn't kind at all. She was just trying to take my best friend away from me. I didn't have a clue what kitten heels were anyway. It was a silly name. Kittens pad about on little fluffy paws. They don't *wear* heels.

I asked Mum and she described them very carefully.

'Why, Gemma? You don't want a pair of kitten heels, do you? You're much too young for any kind of heels, but it would be good for you to have a change from those awful old trainers,' Mum said eagerly.

'*Mum!* I don't want kitten heels.' I paused. 'I *do* want a big sparkly suit though.'

Mum sighed. 'Not again, Gemma. I'm not having my daughter going round in drag!'

'You sometimes wear trouser suits to work, Mum. Does that mean *you* wear drag?'

'No it doesn't, Miss Cheeky Face,' said Mum. She tweaked my hair, sighing. 'It's sticking straight up, even worse than usual, Gemma! What have you been doing to it?'

I'd been raking my hands through it while I read Alice's latest e-mail but I wasn't going to tell Mum that. I let her brush my hair into submission.

'There! It can look quite nice if you just take a bit of care with it. It could look really stunning if we grew it.'

'I was thinking I'd actually like it a bit shorter, Mum,' I said. Fat Larry had a very short haircut. Ideally I wanted a shaved-head skinhead special but I knew Mum would go bananas at the very idea.

I was going to have serious problems with my Fat Larry impersonation, but I couldn't give up. I knew I could be brilliant as Fat Larry. Well. So long as I could cook a bit too.

I smiled at Mum, fluttering my eyelids winsomely.

'Have you got something in your eyes, Gemma?'

'No, no. They're fine. Mum . . . I'm sorry I'm not more of a girly-type girl like Alice. I wish you could kind of help me do girly stuff.'

141

Mum blinked back at me. 'Oh, Gemma darling! Of course I'll help you. I could show you exactly how to do your hair. Maybe we could manicure your nails a little, they're always so grimy. And you could go back to your ballet class and—'

'*Not* ballet, Mum! But could I learn to cook? I'd really really really love to do cookery. Will you show me how to do stuff? *Please?*'

'Well, I don't think we'll tackle pancakes just yet,' said Mum. 'But I'd love to show you how to cook. Come on, you can help me make supper. We're having cauliflower cheese.'

'Oh yuck, Mum. I *hate* cauliflower cheese. Can't we have spag bol?'

'Gemma, you really are the limit. You're the only one in our family who can still stomach the very idea of spaghetti bolognese and yet *you* were the one who vomited it all over everywhere.' Mum shuddered at the memory. 'We're having cauliflower cheese, like it or lump it.'

That was half the reason I disliked it – all those soggy smelly *lumpy* bits of cauliflower swimming around in cheese sauce. I was sure it didn't figure in Fat Larry's recipe book, but at least it was a kind of cookery and I needed the practice.

Mum set me grating the cheese while she washed and cut up the cauliflower. I had to grate a *lot* of cheese. I had a quick nibble at the big wedge in my hand whenever I thought Mum wasn't looking. She caught me chewing. She gave me this long lecture.

'Mum, it's a well-known fact, all good chefs taste their own food. It's part of the creative culinary process,' I said grandly, daring one last weeny bite.

'Stop it! I don't want your teethmarks all over the cheese, you mucky little girl. And chefs taste their food after they've cooked it, not when it's still raw ingredients. Now get on with the grating, I shall want to start the sauce in a second.'

I grated. And grated. And grated. I tried to build up a rhythm. Then I started making up my own rap tune, banging the grater in time.

'This is the way I grate the cheese.
This is the way I make Mum please.
This is the way I shoot the breeze.
This is the way I pay my fees.
This is the way I knock my knees.
This is the way I buzz the bees.
This is the way I rattle my keys.
This is the way I scratch my fleas.
This is the way I widdle my wees—'

'*Gemma!*' said Mum.

She made me jump. I grated my thumb instead of the cheese. It bled rapidly over my pile of cheese gratings, dyeing it an interesting shade of scarlet.

143

Mum had to throw my bloody cheese away and start all over again with a fresh pound of cheddar.

I watched, waggling my sticking-plastered sore thumb.

'What can I do, Mum, if you won't let me carry on grating?'

'You can clear off, Gemma. Please. You can lay the table if you truly want to be helpful.'

'That's not cookery! Oh please, Mum, let me do something. Go on, you're always nagging at me to take an interest in girly stuff, and now I *am* you're giving me no encouragement whatsoever.'

Mum sighed – but when she'd finished her grating she showed me how to make cheese sauce. I tried to learn it by heart. I was still in rap mode.

'Melt the butter,
My mum did utter.
Stir in the flour,
Hour by hour,
Pour on the milk,
Stir smooth as silk,
In with the cheese,
That's the way to please . . .'
I chanted, dancing round the kitchen floor.

I was the all-singing, all-dancing cook. Maybe I'd get my own TV show and be just as popular as Fat

Larry. I'd be Jolly Joking Gemma, top of the telly ratings, rapping her recipes, tapping her cookery tips.

I whirled round, flinging my arms wide as I acknowledged rapturous applause from the studio audience. My gesture was a little too flamboyant. I knocked Mum's arm and the saucepan went flying . . .

I ended up in deep disgrace *again*. I didn't really fancy my cauliflower cheese when we started in on it quite a long while later.

'I take it our Gem's pants at cookery?' Dad murmured to Mum as he set off for work. The shouting from the kitchen had echoed all over the house.

Mum sniffed. 'It's not funny. She's not allowed in my kitchen while I'm cooking, *ever again*!'

'Nice one, Gem,' said Callum, grinning at me.

I didn't have the heart to grin back. I was starting to agree with Mum. It wasn't funny at all. How was I ever going to practise my cookery if she wasn't even going to let me in the kitchen? I decided I'd have to beg Grandad to let me practise round at his place.

I suffered through school the next day. Biscuits was unbearable, going on about his Fat Larry sparkly suit. *His* mum had gone up to London looking for exactly the right sort of sparkly material. Fat Larry specialized in traffic-light colours and had a red suit, a yellow suit and an emerald green.

'I'm going for emerald,' Biscuits boasted.

'Oh, like you think you'll make *me* green with envy?' I said. 'OK, I'll go for a red Fat Larry suit and you'll be red with rage.'

'Look, stop being daft. You know I'm going to be Fat Larry. I *look* like him.'

'I'll look like him too.'

'But you don't have a sparkly suit.'

'I will have. My mum's going to make one.'

'Well, she'll have to get a move on. Didn't you listen? We're presenting the projects the week after next, Mrs Watson said. And there's a prize for the best one.'

'That's ages away,' I said airily, but I started to panic inside. I'd have to watch Fat Larry videos every day and try very hard with my cooking.

I tore out of school to meet Grandad.

'Hello, Iced Gem. What are you in such a hurry for?' said Grandad, taking my hand.

'I want to watch Fat Larry and do some serious cooking before Mum comes to pick me up at your house, Grandad,' I said.

'Oh help!' said Grandad. 'Fat Larry watching is fine, but I'm not so sure about the serious cookery bit. Your dad phoned me today. I don't want you grating away any more fingers, OK?' He gently squeezed my plastered thumb.

'I've got to practise somehow, Grandad. Do you

think I could come round at the weekend and we could learn to cook together then?'

'I'm busy at the weekend, sweetheart,' said Grandad, with a strange smile on his face.

'Grandad, *please*!'

'No – can't, darling. I've got a special job.'

'Oh bum,' I said. 'I wish you didn't have your bogging job.'

'Language, language! It's quite a good job, sweetheart. Particularly this weekend special. Some old lady's hurt her leg on a visit to her daughter and she needs to be collected and taken down to her other daughter in London. She won't fly and she can't take the train because her leg needs to be propped up. She's decided to do the journey in comfort, so I'm picking her up in the Mercedes.'

I wondered why Grandad was rambling on about this old lady at such length.

'Guess where she lives, Gemma!' said Grandad, eyes gleaming. 'Eastern Scotland – about forty or fifty miles away from Alice's new place. So I thought what we could do is pop you in the car and take you on a little trip too. If we drive up Friday night then you could spend all Saturday with Alice. Would you like that?'

'Oh Grandad!' I said.

I leaped up and threw my arms round his neck, hugging him tight.

Thirteen

I was so excited I felt I was skimming the pavement, tap-dancing in thin air.

Then Mum stuck her oar in.

'Your grandad's gone soft in the head. You can't go all the way to Scotland and back in a weekend. And this old lady won't want you in the car, Gemma, it's just ludicrous. And Karen will object strongly if you turn up on her doorstep. I know she thinks you're a bad influence on Alice, and you *are*.'

I felt like Mum had a real oar in her hand and was whacking me over the head with it. I came down to earth. It felt like she was hammering me through the floorboards, down and down and down until my chin was on the carpet.

Dad was dozing on the sofa as always. But then he opened his eyes. He got up. He went over to Mum. 'What's all this?'

She told him. 'Your dad's got no right to start all this. He's got Gemma all worked up. Look at the state of her!'

'*Please* let me go, Mum. Grandad said it would be fine,' I sobbed.

'Never mind your grandad. I'm your mum and I say you're not going.'

Dad picked up his cup of coffee. He took a long sip. 'I think you *should* mind your grandad, Gemma,' he said. 'I'm your dad and I say you *are* going!'

I stared at Dad. Mum stared at him too.

'What on earth are you on about? It's a crazy idea. Your dad's crazy.'

'No he's not. He just can't stand Gemma being so miserable because she's missing young Alice. I don't get your objections. Dad knows what he's doing. He's the safest driver you could wish for. He'll make sure he's well rested. The car hire company will create if they find out about Gemma but if Dad's willing to take that risk I don't see why we should object. She can tuck herself away in a corner of the Merc easily enough. She might even prove good company for this old lady. And yes, we all know our Gemma isn't flavour of the month with snotty old Karen but I doubt she'll have the heart to turn her away if she arrives on the doorstep. Let the kids have one good day together. It can be like an early birthday for them both.'

Dad took a long gulp of coffee. He was probably dry. He wasn't used to saying so much all at one time.

Mum usually said lots and lots but now she

seemed struck dumb. I held my breath.

She looked at Dad. She looked at me. She shook her head. 'It's a mad idea. I have a horrible feeling it'll only end in tears.'

'Look at the kid. She's in tears now,' said Dad. 'We're going to let her go.'

Mum sighed. Then she shrugged. 'All right. I can't fight you both. Gemma can go.'

I shot straight up in the air again, so happy I was bouncing up to the ceiling. I sweet-talked Jack into letting me use his computer right that second, even though he was in the middle of searching for information for some boring old school project about our galaxy.

I thought momentarily about *my* school project but I suddenly didn't care too much. Maybe I'd let Biscuits be Fat Larry after all, seeing as he was fat, he was getting a sparkly suit and he could cook. I couldn't understand why I'd been making such a fuss. I was only fussed about one thing now. *Seeing Alice!*

Hello, Flora. Please give the following Ultra Important message to Alice AS SOON AS HUMANLY POSSIBLE.

Dear Alice, I don't know if you've got anything planned for Saturday but if so, *un*plan it immediately because guess what guess what guess what!!!! My grandad's

150

driving me up to Scotland on Friday night and he's taking me round to your place on Saturday morning. Isn't that WONDERFUL!!! I can't WAIT. But don't tell your mum because she doesn't like me now.

Lots of love from your best friend ever,
Gemma

I hoped the dozy Margarine Girl would nip round to Alice's sharpish but no such luck. I had to wait AGES for a reply. I kept plaguing and plaguing Jack, terrified he might absent-mindedly have deleted my message or mixed it up with his school project and sent it off to some far-flung corner of the galaxy. But *eventually* Alice sent a message back.

Dear Gem,
That is great news! I can't wait to see you. Do you know what time you're coming? And when you're going? The thing is, I usually go to the shops with Mum in the mornings but don't worry I'll say I've got a headache or an earache or something, so I get to stay home. Although if I make too much fuss Mum might make me go to the doctor's. But don't worry, I'll sort something out. Flora will help, she always has good ideas.

Love, Alice

I got a bit bothered by the Flora bit. Why on earth did Alice want to bring her into it? *I* was the one who

151

had good ideas. And *bad* ideas. I'm famous for it.

I had another brilliant idea. Dad had said it would be like an early birthday for both of us, so what we needed was a birthday cake. Then we could blow out our candles together and make our very special best friends for ever birthday wish. Then we were safe for another whole year.

There was a slight problem, however. I didn't know how to make a birthday cake.

I knew a boy who did.

'Hello, Biscuits,' I said the next day at school.

Biscuits blinked back at me nervously. 'What's up?' he said.

'Nothing's up,' I said.

'Then why are you grinning at me like that?'

'Well, we're mates, aren't we?'

'Gemma, have you gone into a time warp? We *were* mates once upon a time. Then all the you-and-Alice business happened and you didn't want to be mates any more. You wanted us to be deadly enemies. You even wanted to beat me up, which was pretty scary, seeing as I'm a Class One Coward. And now we have this uneasy truce because we've been working on our Fat Larry project and—'

'Talking of Fat Larry, Biscuits, you know that yummy chocolate cake you made? That would make an *excellent* birthday cake.'

152

Biscuits sucked his teeth. 'Yeah,' he said thoughtfully.

'Biscuits, do you think you could give me the recipe?'

'Sure,' he said. 'I know it off by heart. OK, here's what you do.'

And then he told me. It was like he was talking another language altogether.

'Hang on,' I said, trying to scribble it down. 'If you've got butter and sugar how do you "cream" them? Do you pour cream on top?'

Biscuits laughed like I was deliberately joking. Then he saw my face. 'Haven't you ever made any kind of cake, Gemma?'

'Well. Not exactly. Not a *cake* sort of cake.'

When we were very little kids Alice and I had mixed up bowls of earth and decorated them with buttercups and daisies and *called* them cakes but they weren't the edible kind.

I had a sudden foreboding that even if I used real ingredients my cake still might not be entirely edible.

'Creaming is easy-peasy,' Biscuits said gently. 'Especially if your mum's got a good food mixer.'

'Mum won't let me loose in her kitchen. I don't think she's got a mixer anyway. She gets my birthday cakes from Marks and Spencer. I'll be making this cake at Grandad's. I don't think he's got a mixer either.'

'Has he got cake tins? And a sieve? And an icing bag to write a message?'

'No. And no. And no again,' I said, sighing.

'Well, come back to my house after school. You can borrow all my mum's stuff. And I'll show you how to make the cake,' said Biscuits.

His face was shining with good will and generosity. I'd been so horrible to him for weeks. I'd even ambushed him in the toilets and tried to beat him up. I'd deliberately insulted him. I'd done my best to stop him impersonating his hero.

He hadn't been mean back once. Biscuits was a truly big-hearted boy.

My own heart seemed to have whittled down to a weeny speck of grit. I could feel it scratch scratch scratching in my chest.

'You're very kind, Biscuits,' I said, in a very small voice.

Biscuits grinned. 'Oh, I don't know. It's kind of fun making you feel guilty,' he said.

I pretended to bop him on the head. He pretended to pull my hair. We shadow-sparred for a minute, elaborating on the theme, miming kick boxing and kung fu, until we were both helpless with laughter.

154

Mrs Watson came into the classroom and found us collapsed in a heap, feebly poking each other with our little fingers.

'Are you two fighting?' she said uncertainly.

'This is a deadly dual of finger prodding, Mrs Watson,' I said. 'Only it's hard to prod Biscuits properly because he's so fa— so big and strong and muscly.'

'Quite,' said Mrs Watson. 'Well, delightful though it is to see you two united in your unusual combat, I rather think you're here to *learn*. Jump up, both of you, and go to your desks, otherwise *I* shall start prodding you – and I'll use my ruler!'

When Grandad came to meet me after school I asked if I could go home with Biscuits to learn cake-making.

'You can come too,' Biscuits said to Grandad.

'It's very kind of you, lad, but you don't want me tagging along too,' said Grandad.

'Oh yes we do!' I said. 'You can learn cake-making too, Grandad. Biscuits makes wonderful cakes. I bet Fat Larry himself couldn't make better.'

'Biscuits looks a dead ringer for your Fat Larry pal too,' said Grandad. 'Why on earth isn't *he* acting the part for this school project of yours?'

There was a little pause. I took a deep breath.

'Yeah, Grandad. You've got a good point. OK, Biscuits. You be Fat Larry when we do the presentation.'

Biscuits nibbled at his lip ruminatively. 'I think we should *both* be Fat Larry somehow. That would be fairer,' he said. He persuaded Grandad to come back to his place too.

'Well, if you're sure your mum won't mind,' said Grandad. 'And talking of mums, Gem, we'd better phone your mum to let her know where we are.'

He phoned Mum at work. I could tell she was giving him an earful on the other end of the phone, probably quizzing him about Biscuits and his family. Grandad pressed the phone close to his ear and mumbled, 'Yes, Liz, no, Liz,' several times. Then he mouthed, 'Three bags full, Liz,' so that I got the giggles.

On the way to Biscuits' house Grandad suggested we wait by the gate, rather than going straight in. 'That way you can nip in, lad, and check with your mum if it's convenient,' said Grandad. He rubbed his ear as if my mum's voice was still quacking away at him.

'Oh, my mum will be fine,' said Biscuits. 'She likes me bringing friends home.'

'Yeah, but maybe she won't like me,' I said. '*Some* mums don't like me one bit.'

But Mrs McVitie gave me a great big smile when she opened her front door.

'This is Gemma, Mum,' said Biscuits eagerly.

156

'Of course it is,' said Mrs McVitie. 'I've heard a lot about you, sweetheart.' She smiled at Grandad. 'And are you Gemma's dad?'

'Her *gran*dad!'

'Well I never. You don't look old enough to be a grandad,' said Mrs McVitie.

She was just teasing him but Grandad looked really chuffed.

Everyone smiled in the McVitie family. Mr McVitie smiled when he came home from work at his barber's shop. He ruffled my hair and asked me if I'd just had it cut.

'No, I'm supposed to be growing it. I don't want to, though. I want it really really short. I don't suppose you'd give me a skinhead number one, would you?'

Mr McVitie roared with laughter. 'I don't think your mum would be too thrilled about that, darling. I think you'd better confer with her first.'

I decided to put the idea on hold for a while.

Biscuits' granny smiled as she made us all a cup of tea. She gave Grandad his in a mug that said HUNKY GUY. Grandad had a little chuckle about it. He'd been going to take a cookery lesson with me but he ended up sitting on the sofa with the granny,

looking at her photograph album. Both of them hooted with laughter at the things they all wore back in the Old Days.

Biscuits' baby sister Polly smiled too, lying back in her baby chair, waving her little clenched fists and kicking her plump pink legs. Biscuits was *brilliant* with her, parking her baby chair up on top of the kitchen table beside us so she could see what we were doing. He chatted away to her like she was a real little person, tickling her under her chin and playing 'This Little Piggy' with her tiny toes. Polly squealed delightedly, blinking her blue eyes at her big brother.

I wondered if Callum had ever played with me like that. I was certain *Jack* wouldn't have gone anywhere near me. Little babies freak him out.

I'm not usually very keen on babies either. I politely said Polly was very sweet. I couldn't say she was *pretty* because she was much too pink and piggly and totally bald.

'I'll take her out of her baby chair and let you hold her, if you like,' said Biscuits.

'No fear!' I said hurriedly. 'I'd probably drop her.'

Mum was always going on about me being so rough and clumsy. I had a little knot in my stomach already in case I made a complete mess of cake-making. I *did* sift my flour a little too vigorously so that it looked like there was a mini snowstorm in the kitchen but Biscuits just laughed. *His mum laughed too!*

Biscuits showed me how to sift sensibly. Then he demonstrated the complicated creaming lark. The butter and sugar went into this unpromising gritty ball at first but it smoothed out eventually, and really went creamy. Then Biscuits initiated me into the very *best* bit about cake-making – licking out the bowl!

Grandad tried to pay for all the cake ingredients but Mrs McVitie wouldn't hear of it. Grandad promised the whole family a free trip out the next time his work Mercedes was available.

'Only it can't be this weekend. I'm taking a very special little lady on a long long trip up North,' he said, winking at me.

'You're going to see Alice?' said Biscuits.

'Yep! Won't that be wonderful?' I said.

'Well. I suppose. And so this cake's for *her*?' said Biscuits.

'It's for us to share. An early birthday cake. So

159

when it comes out the oven, will you show me how to ice it over and do fancy writing on the top?'

'OK.'

'I want quite a lot of writing. *Alice and Gemma, Best Friends For Ever*. Will it fit?'

'Probably.'

Biscuits seemed to have got a bit fed up with cake-making. He filled the icing bag for me to have a practice on greased paper while the cake was baking. Then he turned his back on me and made a great fuss of Polly. He pulled funny faces at her and she chortled appreciatively.

I tried to master writing in icing. It wasn't easy. The loopy bits wobbled and the round bits blotched.

Biscuits started playing peekaboo with Polly. Every time he went 'Boo' my hand shook and my words went wrong.

'Oh bum,' I said, and then glanced anxiously at Mrs McVitie.

She was busy washing up and didn't hear, thank goodness.

'I can't do it!' I wailed.

'Yes you can,' said Biscuits. 'Keep practising.'

'I *am*. Help me, Biscuits. Hold the bag with me and show me again. Please!'

Biscuits sighed but he came over, put his big hands round mine and squeezed smoothly on the

160

bag. I let him choose the words. He wrote:

Gemma is rubbish at icing.

'OK, OK,' I said, struggling to take over. 'Well, give it me back. I'll have another go.'

I wrote alone, slowly, wobbling all over the place:

Biscuits is a great mate.

Biscuits' smile came back.
He smiled and smiled and smiled.

Fourteen

It was great fun riding along in the Mercedes. Grandad kept calling me Lady Gemma and asking me if I'd like a drink or a sweet or a rug around my knees. We stopped at a motorway café around six o'clock. We both had a huge fry-up of sausages, bacon, baked beans and chips. Grandad let me squirt tomato sauce out of a squeezy bottle all over mine. I wanted to write

Yummy nosh!

but it took up too much room, so I settled for

Yum!

When we got back on the road Grandad tuned into a Golden Oldie radio channel and sang me all these old songs, telling me how he used to jive to them with Grandma. I sang too, but when the radio frequency started to fade I faded too.

I curled up on the comfy leather seat, head on a cushion, rug wrapped around me, and slept deeply for hours and hours. Then I was vaguely aware Grandad was picking me up, still wrapped up in the rug like a big baby in a shawl. He was carrying me into a dark house and tucking me up in a little camp bed.

I went straight back to sleep. When I woke up it was a bright sunny morning and I was in a totally strange bedroom, Grandad gently snoring over in the big bed.

I got up and had a little wander round the room. I peeped out of the curtains, expecting to see mountains and lochs and hairy Highland cattle and men in tartan kilts. It was disappointing to see a perfectly ordinary street of grey houses and a video shop and a newsagent and a Chinese takeaway just like at home. There was a man coming out of the newsagent's with his paper and a pint of milk but he was wearing trousers, and they weren't even tartan.

'What are you looking at, sweetheart?' Grandad mumbled.

'Scotland. But it doesn't look very foreign,' I said.

'You wait till I drive you to Alice's new house. It's right out in the country.'

'Can we go now?'

'Soon. After we've had breakfast.'

It was a satisfyingly *Scottish* breakfast cooked by Mrs Campbell, the lady who ran the boarding house. We had our breakfast in a special dining room with the other guests. Grandad and I had our own little table for two. I plucked at the checked tablecloth.

'Is this tartan?' I asked.

'Aye, it is indeed, lassie. The Campbell tartan, I expect. They're a very grand clan – especially the ladyfolk,' said Grandad, putting on a very bad Scottish accent.

Mrs Campbell didn't mind. She giggled at Grandad and gave us extra big helpings of porridge.

'You're supposed to eat your porridge with salt when you're in Scotland,' said Grandad.

'He can have the salt, darling, but *you* can have brown sugar and cream,' said Mrs Campbell, giving me a little bowl and jug. 'But leave room for your smokies.'

I wasn't sure what smokies were. They turned out to be lovely cooked fish swimming in butter. Mrs Campbell cut mine off the bone for me. Then she brought us lots of toast with a special pot of Dundee marmalade.

'I *like* Scotland,' I said.

'Me too,' said Grandad, patting his stomach.

'Hey, maybe *we* could live up here, Grandad. Just you and me. You could drive a car round here and I could go to Alice's school. It would be brilliant! I could keep house for you, Grandad. I'm getting to be a great cook. Biscuits' mum said my cake was absolutely tip-top, didn't she? I could make you a cake every single day. Wouldn't that be wonderful?'

'What about your mum and dad and Callum and Jack and that mad dog?'

'Oh, I expect I'd miss them a little bit, but I'd *much* sooner be with you and see Alice.'

'Let's just deal with today first. I can't cope with long-term plans, not on a full stomach,' said Grandad. 'Now, hush a minute while I have a look at the map. I've got to work out exactly how to get to Alice's.'

It took longer than we'd thought. We drove right out into the countryside. Just as Grandad had promised, there were great stark mountains and blue lochs. I stared at field after field with perfectly ordinary cows – and then I suddenly spotted a fat hairy orange creature with horns.

I screamed excitedly and Grandad swerved and swore.

'For heaven's sake, Gem, *what*? I nearly crashed the car!'

'A Highland cow! Look, Grandad, it really is!'

165

'Oh goodie, goodie!' said Grandad sarcastically, mopping his brow. But then he smiled at me. 'Sorry, sweetheart. I didn't mean to be grumpy. It's just . . . I'm beginning to wonder if your mum might have been right all along. I think I must be going nuts. What if Alice is out when we get there?'

'She won't be, Grandad, I promise,' I said happily.

'How can you be so sure?' said Grandad.

'Trust me,' I said.

'Well, supposing they *are* in, what if her mum and dad won't let you see her? They were so cross with you two for running away like that.'

'Grandad, even Auntie Karen isn't going to tell us to bog off when we've driven hundreds of bogging miles.'

'Hey, hey, you'll have to watch that mouth of yours, little girl.'

'OK, OK. Don't look so worried, Grandad. Everything will be lovely, lovely, lovely.'

'Yes, but just suppose Alice isn't quite as pleased to see you as you'd like?'

I stared at Grandad. It was as if he'd started talking a foreign language. He wasn't making any kind of sense. Maybe he really was starting to go a little bit nuts.

'Of *course* Alice will be pleased to see me,' I said.

We found their village eventually. We drove round

it twice asking for directions and going up the wrong lane and round the wrong corner but *finally* we juddered the car down a long grassy trail with big trees and bushes on either side. We turned a corner into a clearing and there was the house.

It was an amazing house too! I understood why Auntie Karen had got so excited about it. It was a big grey stone building, practically a palace, with lots of leaded windows and a large studded wooden front door. It was like one of those huge houses where you pay to have a guided tour.

'This can't be Alice's house,' I said.

'Blooming heck! They've certainly gone up in the world,' said Grandad. 'It must be their house though, because that's Alice's dad's car in the driveway.'

'Look up at the top window! There's Melissa on the windowsill – see all her long ringlets?' Then I spotted another head. 'And there's *Alice*!'

She looked out of the window and saw Grandad and me down below in the car. She disappeared. Within seconds the large front door opened and Alice came hurtling out.

'Gemma!'

'Oh Ali, Ali, Ali!' I shouted, jumping out of the Mercedes.

Then we were hugging each other hard, whirling round and round, laughing and crying all at the same time.

'You two!' said Grandad, mopping at his own eyes.

'Have you told your mum and dad?' I asked Alice.

'I've told *Dad*,' said Alice.

Uncle Bob came out of the house. I was so used to seeing him in posh suits I hardly recognized him. He was all dressed up for his new country life in a checked shirt and a big quilty waistcoat and cord trousers and gumboots. He looked such a total wally in his green welly get-up that I burst out laughing. Luckily he just thought I was laughing because I was so happy to see Alice. He patted me on the head and shook hands with Grandad, saying it was frightfully good of him to drive all this way. He looked at the Mercedes in astonishment.

'New car?' he said weakly.

Grandad was chuckling too. 'I fancied a bit of comfort in my old age,' he said. 'Well, I've got all sorts of stuff to attend to. Is it OK if I leave young Gemma here and come and collect her around tea time?'

'Of course, of course,' said Uncle Bob, but he looked anxious when Auntie Karen started calling.

'Alice? Bob? Where have you two got to?'

She came out the front door, wearing very tight white trousers and a white fluffy sweater. Her face went white too when she saw me. 'Gemma! You dreadful girl, you've not run away *again*?'

Then she saw Grandad. Her pale face flushed pink. 'I'm sorry, I didn't mean . . .'

'She *is* a dreadful girl, we all know that,' said Grandad, putting his arm round me. 'But I'm to blame this time. I had to come up to Scotland on business so I brought young Gemma with me. I hope she can stay and play with Alice today?'

'Well, we *were* going out—' Auntie Karen started.

'Oh Mum! I have to make the most of every *minute* of Gemma,' said Alice.

'Gemma promises to be as good as gold, don't you, Sweet Pea?' said Grandad.

'Yes, don't worry, Auntie Karen, I'm on my absolutely best behaviour.'

169

'Well, maybe you can stay for lunch.'

'Oh Mum! Gemma's got to stay for tea too.'

'But the Hamiltons are coming. I'm not sure we'll have enough . . .' said Auntie Karen.

'Oh, that's fine, Auntie Karen, we'll have heaps because I've brought a cake. I made it all myself – well, nearly, didn't I, Grandad?'

'Yes, you did, pet. But maybe you'd better not stay if it's going to be a bother,' said Grandad, frowning.

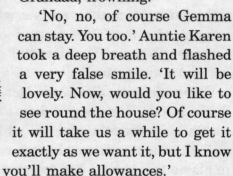

'No, no, of course Gemma can stay. You too.' Auntie Karen took a deep breath and flashed a very false smile. 'It will be lovely. Now, would you like to see round the house? Of course it will take us a while to get it exactly as we want it, but I know you'll make allowances.'

Grandad got roped into this Grand Tour. He wiped his shoes carefully as he stepped into the hall and made a big effort, remarking on the big airy rooms and the wonderful thick carpets and the dazzling light fittings and the beautiful views from the windows. Every time Auntie Karen looked away Grandad pulled a funny face and mopped his brow.

Alice skipped ahead. 'Wait till you see my bedroom, Gemma, just wait!' she kept calling.

We had to see Auntie Karen and Uncle Bob's bedroom first, plus their ensuite bathroom. Auntie Karen even demonstrated their power shower, splashing us a little bit so that Grandad had to wipe his glasses.

'And this is the guest room,' said Auntie Karen, opening the next door. Then she bit her lip and closed it again. 'We haven't fixed it up properly. We haven't even got a proper spare bed,' she said.

I'm pretty certain Auntie Karen was fibbing. She just wanted to make sure she wasn't landed with *us* as guests.

'Now I'll show you Alice's bedroom,' she said.

'About time,' said Alice, taking me by the hand and pulling me inside.

I'd wiped my shoes too but I wondered if I should take them off altogether. Alice had a pale-pink carpet with a deep-pink rug in the shape of a rose beside her bed. She had a new duvet cover, white with pink roses, and frilly matching curtains. She had the same wardrobe and chest of drawers but they'd been painted rose pink to match the rug. Alice had a brand new pinkly-painted desk with a pink fluffy notebook and pencil case and several pink gel pens laid out neatly on top.

Pink

pink

(white and) pink

pink

'It's very . . . pink,' I said.

I looked at Melissa on the windowsill. My heart started beating fast. 'She's wearing a pink dress,' I said.

Alice smiled. 'Yes, doesn't she look lovely? Flora gave it to me. She had this modern china doll called Miss Rosepetal and we swapped outfits. Melissa matches my bedroom now.'

I swallowed. I glanced at Grandad but he was wearily complimenting Auntie Karen on her flower stencilling and hadn't even noticed.

Melissa looked awful in her sleazy pink ruffles. I badly wanted to dress her back in her own white frock but I felt I couldn't make a fuss, not now I was on my very best behaviour.

Alice didn't seem to have any idea that I minded about Melissa's outfit. That was weird too, because we always knew exactly what the other was thinking. Alice happily showed me all her new fancy pink treasures. She even had a new pink dressing gown and a pink nightie with grown-up straps.

'I put it on and pretend it's an evening dress and play pop stars,' said Alice. 'Isn't it glorious? Dead sexy!' She held it up against herself and twirled around, doing this silly wiggly dance.

'No, *this* is dead sexy,' I said, strutting around

172

on my toes, pretending to be this lap-dancer I'd once seen on television before Mum switched it off sharpish.

'What *are* you playing at, Gemma?' said Auntie Karen.

'Hey, hey, that's enough, our Gem,' said Grandad. 'I thought you were supposed to be on your best behaviour? Now don't you go letting yourself down or Auntie Karen won't let you stay and play with Alice.'

'No, no, of course she can stay. Until tea time. No – *after* tea, of course. It will be lovely. For Alice.'

Grandad said he'd better be on his way as he had all sorts of errands to do. I gave him a big hug. I had this sudden weird feeling that I didn't want him to leave me. I didn't know what was the matter with me. It meant all the world to me to be with Alice, and yet suddenly I wasn't quite sure about her. It was as if *she'd* been painted bright pink and dressed in frills.

Grandad went to get the cake out of the car and gave the tin to Auntie Karen. She stayed downstairs in the kitchen, preparing for her tea party. Uncle Bob whistled outside in the garden. Alice and I were left on our own together.

I looked at her. She looked at me.

'So . . . you like my bedroom?' said Alice.

'Yes, it's beautiful,' I said.

I sat down very gingerly on the end of her bed. Alice sat beside me.

'And you like all my new stuff?'

'Everything's lovely. Though how terrible to lose Golden Syrup!'

'Oh, he was so old and scruffy. I like my ballet bear *much* better. I'm getting all sorts of new stuff. Mum says I might be able to have my own television.'

'A fluffy pink one?' I said.

'I don't think they make them like that,' said Alice, taking me seriously.

'Why don't you ask for your own computer? Then we could e-mail each other direct without having to get that Flora involved.'

'Flora doesn't mind. She's been ever so sweet about it,' said Alice. 'You'll meet her this afternoon, Gemma. She's coming to tea with her mum and dad.'

'But – but you knew *I* was coming,' I said.

'Yes, but my mum invited them, see. You'll *like* Flora, she's great.'

'I thought it would be kind of like a birthday tea for you and me.'

'But it's weeks until our birthday.'

'Still, I made a cake, so we could have our birthday wish.'

'A *real* cake?'

'Yeah. You wait till you see it.'

'Gem, you can't cook.'

'I can. Biscuits helped me.'

'Oh yuck! I don't want a cake made by Biscuits.'

'He's a good cook. He watches Fat Larry. We're doing a project about him at school.'

'What a weird project! Hey, do you want to see Flora's and my Egyptian project? She's done most of the writing and I've done the pictures. You draw ancient Egyptians sideways and I'm good at noses.'

'Do you think the ancient Egyptians walked sideways in real life?' I said, jumping up and demonstrating.

'Don't be daft, Gem. Look – see my picture of an Egyptian mummy. The hieroglyphics took me *ages*. I've used special gold pencil all round the edges to show it's a mummy of someone really royal and special.'

'Is it a man or a woman?'

'You can't always tell. They all seemed to wear black eye make-up.'

'Maybe it's a trick mummy. When you open it up you find another decorated mummy inside, and then another and another – you know, like those wooden Russian dolls – and then *eventually* you find a weeny *baby* mummy, and its hierowhatsits will be pictures of bunnies and storks and fluffy ducklings.'

'Oh Gemma!' said Alice, but she started giggling.

'Look, I've drawn a cat mummy too. You reminded me about them. They look so weird all stretched out like that. I wonder if they turned any other animals into mummies. Imagine a cow mummy! They'd have a job squashing its legs into place. It would look weird, a long squeezed-out neck and then a head with horns. Hey, imagine a *giraffe* mummy – its neck would go on for ever!'

'I don't think they *have* giraffes in Egypt,' said Alice, but she'd really got the giggles now.

I wound myself up in her duvet and stuck my head out, my eyes bulging, pretending to be a giraffe mummy. Alice laughed so much she had to flop on her bed.

'Oh Gemma, I have missed you so. You're such *fun.*'

We had fun all morning, messing around in Alice's bedroom. It was as if all the pinkness had peeled away and we were back in her old bedroom at home.

I got a bit tense again when Auntie Karen called us for lunch. I always seem to spill more than usual when I'm anxious. But it wasn't a formal knife-and-fork sit-up-properly-at-the-table kind of lunch. She'd fixed us hot dogs and crisps and salad on blue plastic picnic plates. Auntie Karen just had the salad.

'Don't you like hot dogs, Auntie Karen?' I asked.

'I prefer to stick with salad,' said Auntie Karen, though she didn't look as if she was relishing her carrot shreds and lettuce.

'She's on this silly diet,' said Uncle Bob. 'Though I can't think why you want to lose weight. You look splendid to me.' He gave her a pretend smack on her big white bottom.

'Bob! Stop it!' Auntie Karen snapped, but she didn't seem to mind too much.

Uncle Bob pulled a face at Alice and me and we giggled.

Auntie Karen had special squirty tomato sauce to flavour the hot dogs. It was very tempting. I wrote *Gemma* in bright-red writing over my hot dog. Alice tried to write *Alice* on hers but she was far more wobbly.

'How come you're so good at it, Gem?'

'I've been practising. Wait till you see our cake at tea time,' I said, hugging myself.

If only I'd asked for us to have my special birthday tea then! But Auntie Karen gave us both vanilla ice cream with whipped cream and nuts and tinned cherries. We counted our cherry stones.

'Tinker, tailor, soldier, sailor, *rich man* – goodie

goodie,' said Alice. She hid her last cherry stone under her plate because she didn't want it to come out *poor man*.

'Who are you going to marry, Gemma? Oh, poor you – *beggar man*!'

'I think it might be quite good fun to marry a beggar man and be a beggar lady. We could have one of those scrawny beggar dogs and busk.' I picked up a leftover hot dog and hummed, pretending to be playing a harmonica.

I forgot about the tomato sauce.

'Gemma! You look like you've got lipstick all round your mouth,' said Alice, trying to wipe me with her napkin.

'Hey, maybe it's *blood* and I'm a secret vampire and you look so tempting I've taken a secret nip at your lily-white neck,' I said, baring my teeth and bobbing my head at her.

Alice squealed.

Uncle Bob laughed.

Auntie Karen frowned. 'Not at the table, Gemma,' she said.

Her mouth kept going into odd shapes because she had a shred of carrot stuck in her tooth and she was trying to hook it out with her tongue. My own tongue ached to imitate her but I knew I was already getting right up Auntie Karen's nose. I dared one

weeny wobble of my tongue when Auntie Karen
went to the fridge to get some fizzy water.

Alice was taking a long drink of Coke at the time.
She snorted terribly. Coke sprayed out of her nose
in an impressive fountain.

'Gemma!' said Auntie Karen, not looking round.

'Wrong culprit!' said Uncle Bob, patting Alice on
the back.

'Oh *Alice*!' Look, it's all over your DKNY T-shirt.
You'll have to change as we've got the Hamiltons
coming.'

I frowned, absent-mindedly wiping scarlet saucy
fingers over my own ordinary GAP T-shirt.

I wished the Hamiltons weren't invited. I
especially wished wished wished Flora wasn't
coming.

Fifteen

My heart sank when I saw Flora. She was exactly as I'd imagined, only more so. She had long blonde hair gently waving way past her shoulders, big blue eyes and pale creamy skin like rose petals. She was daintily skinny, with a delicate neck and pointy elbows, but her long legs had shapely dancer's calves. She wasn't wearing anything fancy, just a T-shirt and shorts, but the T-shirt was small enough to show off her flat tummy and the shorts were the sort you'd wear to a disco, not the baggy kind that make your bottom look saggy.

'This is Flora, Gemma,' Alice said. She pronounced her flowery name as if it was very special. She was looking at Flora as if she was a princess and Alice was her little serving maid.

Auntie Karen was dancing similar attendance on Flora's mum. She was like Flora but in full bloom. Uncle Bob couldn't stop looking at her too. She was wearing white trousers very similar to

Auntie Karen's but she looked very different in them. Uncle Bob looked as if he was longing to pat her bottom too.

He managed to avert his eyes just long enough to look at Flora's dad and offer him a beer. Auntie Karen tutted irritably and said she'd made a special jug of Pimm's for everyone. I didn't know what Pimm's was but it looked very pretty, like dark lemonade with lots of fruit and mint leaves bobbing about like little boats.

My throat was very dry. I swallowed hopefully, even though there were only four glasses standing beside the jug. It was a very *big* jug. I watched Auntie Karen carefully pouring. She only used up half the lemonade stuff.

'Please may I have a little Pimm's too, Auntie Karen?' I asked, careful to say it very politely.

Auntie Karen sighed as if I was being deliberately cheeky. 'Don't be ridiculous, Gemma,' she said.

Auntie Karen raised her eyebrows at Flora's mum. Flora sniggered.

'I don't know what's so funny,' I said.

'Pimm's is *alcoholic*,' said Flora. 'Surely everyone knows that.' She dug Alice in the ribs. Alice giggled.

'Of course I know that Pimm's is a little bit alcoholic,' I said, sticking my chin in the air. 'I happen to be *allowed* to drink alcohol.'

181

'As if your mother would ever allow any such thing!' said Auntie Karen.

'I didn't say my mother. I frequently have a lager with my *grandad*,' I said.

I wasn't *exactly* telling whopping great fibs. Grandad had let me have one sip out of his can once, just so I could see what it tasted like. It tasted *horrible*, as a matter of fact.

Uncle Bob burst out laughing. 'You're a caution, Gemma,' he said.

'That's one word for her,' said Auntie Karen. 'Now, I've made you girls a jug of real lemonade. Take it down to the end of the garden and leave us in peace. You carry the tray, Flora. I know you'll be careful.'

We went out into the garden in procession, Flora first, bearing the tray of clinking glasses, Alice scurrying second with the jug carefully clutched against her chest, and me trailing in the rear, not trusted to carry anything at all.

The end of the garden had exciting possibilities. There were so many bushes we were mostly out of sight of the grown-ups sitting on the green garden furniture. The grass grew tuftily around our ankles here, and big white weedy flowers grew as high as our heads.

182

'We could play jungles, Alice,' I said excitedly.

'*Play* jungles?' said Flora.

'Gemma's good at pretend games,' said Alice quickly.

Flora blinked her blue eyes rapidly in a silly way to express astonishment. 'I haven't played pretend games for years!' she said. 'Still, you're Alice's guest, Gemma, so I suppose it's polite to let you.'

'I'm not Alice's *guest*, I'm her best friend,' I said fiercely.

'Let's have our lemonade,' said Alice. 'You look very hot, Gem.'

I was burning all over. I could have drunk a lake of lemonade and still been boiling. This was my one and only special day with Alice. Why did Flora have to barge in and start spoiling things? Now we couldn't play any proper games. All Flora seemed to want to do was talk.

She talked about their Egyptian project and how she'd found all this stuff on the internet and printed it out. Alice said she was clever. I said there wasn't really anything *clever* in printing stuff out. I tried to tell them heaps of stuff about the Egyptians but they stopped listening.

Flora talked about ballet and how she'd been picked to do a solo for their end-of-term performance. Alice said she was brilliant. I said I thought ballet was silly and modern dancing was much more fun. I tried twirling and tapping but I tripped and Flora laughed. Alice did too.

Flora talked about her riding lessons and her pony, Nutmeg. Alice said she was lucky, and she couldn't wait to get her own pony too. I said I was getting a white pony called Diamond. As soon as Flora opened her mouth I said I *knew* you called them greys but my Diamond was as white as snow. 'Isn't he, Alice?' I said.

'She hasn't *really* got a pony, has she?' said Flora.

'Well . . .' said Alice.

She didn't say no. She didn't have to.

'Oh, I see – a *pretend* pony,' said Flora, and she clicked her teeth and galloped. She'd never seen me pretending to ride Diamond but she was horribly accurate. 'Neigh!' Flora snorted, tossing her head, trying to make Alice laugh at me again.

Alice bent her head, pulling up a clump of long grass. She started plaiting some strands of it together. Her hair fell over her face so we couldn't see if she was laughing or not. I watched her neat little fingers carefully plaiting.

'What are you making?' said Flora.

I knew what she was making.

'It's just grass jewellery,' said Alice.

It wasn't any old jewellery. It was a friendship bracelet. I held my breath as she finished plaiting. Then she looked up and smiled at me. She wound it round my wrist and tied up the ends. I took hold of her hand and we squeezed each other's thumbs.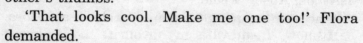

'That looks cool. Make me one too!' Flora demanded.

Alice obediently made her one. It turned out bigger and better this time because she used longer grass and she divided it more evenly, but I didn't care. I had the *first* bracelet. The real friendship bracelet.

'Let's go and dress up in all your real jewellery, Alice,' said Flora. 'Can I wear the silver charm bracelet?'

What did *she* know about Alice's jewellery? And how could she ever think she could wear *my* favourite charm bracelet with the little silver Noah's Ark? I felt as if the weeny giraffes and elephants and tigers were biting me with tiny razor-sharp teeth.

Alice dithered when we were upstairs in her bedroom. She opened up the jewellery box and watched the little ballet dancer whirl round and round. She ran her fingers through all her treasures, the gold heart on a chain, the tiny baby bracelet, the jade bangle, the silver locket and the Scottie dog sparkly brooch. She tried putting every single one of her rings on one finger, the Russian twisted gold and the garnet and all the Christmas cracker jewellery. She didn't touch the silver charm bracelet.

Flora reached over and snatched it up. 'I just *love* this little bracelet,' she said, flicking each charm. 'I especially love the Noah's Ark. There are tiny little animals inside, Gemma, look.'

'I know,' I said. 'It's my favourite too. *I* always get to wear it when we dress up.'

'I asked first,' said Flora.

Alice looked at me helplessly.

'OK,' I said, shrugging. 'You wear it then, Flora.'

I decided not to mind too much. Alice had made the first friendship bracelet for me. That was what mattered. I was going to wear it for ever and ever.

Alice and Flora decked themselves up in all the jewellery.

'Would you like to wear my pink nightie like a grown-up dance dress, Gemma?' Alice offered.

'No thanks,' I said. 'I hate pink, you know I do.'

I suddenly realized how rude that sounded in the midst of Alice's immensely pink bedroom. 'Pink *clothes*,' I corrected myself. 'Pink's perfect for furniture and curtains and walls and stuff. I just don't go a bundle on pink *dresses*.'

I went over to the windowsill and picked up Melissa. 'She doesn't like them either,' I said, unbuttoning her pink satin frills.

'Careful with Rosebud. She's a very precious antique doll,' said Flora.

'I *know* she is. And what's all this Rosebud rubbish? Her name's Melissa.'

'Yeah but that's a yuck name. Rosebud's much prettier and it matches her rosy dress. I gave it to her specially,' said Flora.

'*I* gave Melissa to Alice specially,' I said, easing her out of the pink frilly dress and dropping it on the carpet. Melissa looked so much happier in her long white drawers and petticoat.

'You couldn't possibly have bought her an antique doll,' said Flora. 'Alice said you and your family are really poor.'

Alice's cheeks went as pink as the rosebud frock. 'I didn't exactly say that, Flora. And Gemma *did* give me the doll. Only I still feel bad about it. Would you like her back now, Gem?'

I struggled, hugging Melissa hard against my chest. It was almost like hugging my grandma. 'It's OK, you can still keep her – but promise she can stay being Melissa. She *hates* the name Rosebud.'

'She's a doll, Gemma. She can't think,' said Flora.

That's all *she* knew. Melissa's dark glass eyes were fixed on Flora, hating and hating her. And I hated her too.

Then Auntie Karen called us to say that tea was ready. She'd laid it all out on the garden table, with a yellow and green checked tablecloth and matching napkins. The food itself picked up the yellow and green theme: cucumber sandwiches, golden slithers of quiche and pizza, green salad, lemon tart and cheesecake.

I looked round anxiously. 'Where's *my* cake, Auntie Karen?'

'Oh yes. Sorry, dear, I forgot,' said Auntie Karen. 'Still, the table's a bit full now. Perhaps we should save it till later.'

'But I won't be here later,' I said. 'Grandad's coming for me soon. *Please* let's have my cake now. We can make room for it, easy-peasy.' I tried demonstrating, moving the plates around.

'All right, all right, *careful*! I'll do it, Gemma,' said Auntie Karen.

She went into the kitchen and brought out my cake on a white plate. It was richly chocolate and resplendent, with *Alice and Gemma* carefully iced over the top and little rosettes all round.

'Oh Gemma!' said Alice. 'It's a wonderful cake!'

'My goodness,' said Auntie Karen. 'Don't tell me you made it yourself, Gemma!'

'It looks very yummy,' said Uncle Bob. He smiled at me encouragingly. 'I think I'll cut myself a great big slice.'

'Oh no! Please! Alice and I have to cut it together,' I said, rushing to stop him.

Auntie Karen sighed. 'Whose little tea party *is* this, Gemma?' she said, raising her eyebrows at Flora's mum again.

'Please can we cut the cake, Mum?' said Alice.

'Oh very well, you girls can cut the cake,' said Auntie Karen. 'Then maybe we'll all be able to eat our tea in peace.'

She took the cake knife . . . and handed it to *Flora*!

'Not Flora!' I said. 'It's just for Alice and me.'

I suppose it sounded horribly spoilt and rude but I couldn't help it. Auntie Karen glared at me.

'Now you're going too far, Gemma. Flora dear, you go ahead and cut the cake.'

'No! No, you don't understand. It's so Alice and I can make a special wish,' I said desperately, elbowing my way nearer my precious cake.

Flora still had the cake knife. She smiled at me. 'I'm going to have *my* special wish first,' she said, and she pressed the knife deep into the creamy chocolate topping.

I couldn't bear it. My hands reached out. They clasped the plate.

'No, Gemma! No!' Alice shouted.

I couldn't stop myself. I picked the cake up and thrust it right in Flora's smug pink face.

Sixteen

'Get in the car,' said Grandad. 'Blooming heck, Gem, you don't do things by halves! You've really done it now. You've really really done it.'

I knew that. I knew Auntie Karen would stab me with her cake knife if I ever came visiting again. I knew Flora would never ever ever let me e-mail Alice now. I knew I couldn't be Alice's best friend any more. I'd acted like such a crazy person she probably looked on me as her worst enemy.

She was mopping Flora up now, still wiping cream out of her eyebrows and chocolate sponge out of her long blonde hair.

'Alice won't want to see me ever again,' I wept.

'I think you're mistaken,' said Grandad, looking round.

There was Alice running out of the house towards us, Melissa in her arms. Auntie Karen was shouting after her furiously, but Alice took no notice.

'Here, Gem,' she panted, thrusting Melissa through the car window at me. 'You have her back.

It's only fair. She's yours. *I* never called her Rosebud. That was just Flora.'

'Al, I'm sorry I chucked the cake at Flora. It was just it was *our* cake and *our* wish.'

'I know. Flora was asking for it. Oh Gem, her face!' Alice suddenly burst out laughing and I did too.

Auntie Karen started running towards us, shouting.

'Uh-oh. Better get going, Gem,' said Grandad.

I leaned right out the window and gave Alice one last hug. 'We're still best friends?' I said, as Grandad drove off.

'Of course we are,' Alice shouted over her shoulder, as Auntie Karen hauled her back into the house.

I sank back on my seat, still giggling.

'You're a very very bad little girl. It's not the slightest bit funny,' said Grandad sternly.

'I know,' I said, holding Melissa tight, burying my nose in her soft silky hair.

I stopped giggling. I started sobbing instead.

'Oh Gemma! Come on, now, darling, I didn't mean to make you cry,' said Grandad, patting my knee.

'It's *me* that's making me cry, Grandad. You've been lovely to me and arranged this trip specially.

I'm the one who mucked it all up. I always do. I can't seem to *help* it. And even though Alice and I *are* still best friends we'll never ever be able to see each other now. What am I going to *do*?' I started crying harder. 'I know she's Flora's best friend too.'

'What, old Cake Face?' said Grandad.

I snorted through my sobs.

'Not that it's a laughing matter,' said Grandad. 'If your mum got to hear about it she'd hang, draw and quarter you, young Gemma.'

'You won't tell on me, will you, Grandad?'

'What do you take me for?' said Grandad. 'I'm no snitch. Now, listen to me, Gem darling. Maybe Alice has got the right idea. You'll still be her absolutely the-bee's-knees best friend, but she's got the comfort of having Flora Cake Face as her every-day friend. Maybe you should count your blessings that you've got an everyday pal too.'

I blinked at Grandad. 'Who?'

Grandad shook his head at me. 'Who do you *think*? Come on, Gemma, who do you have the most fun with?'

I knew who Grandad was getting at. But I wasn't in the mood for fun.

We were back in our bed and breakfast early to get a good night's sleep before the long journey home the next day. I had a very *bad* night's sleep.

Grandad gave me a very serious talking to before

193

we went to collect Mrs Cholmondly. It was a funny name. It was spelled Chol-mond-ly but for some weirdo reason it was pronounced Chumly.

'Now, you are to behave yourself *utterly* with Mrs C,' said Grandad. 'One complaint from her and I'll be out of my job altogether. Now, Mrs C is a sad old lady. She's hurt her knee so she's probably in a lot of pain and feeling fussed and worried. She might be a bit sharp or snappy with us. You must *not* give her any cheek back. You must try to be understanding. You're basically a very kind little girl. I know you'll try your best.'

Grandad looked so anxious I put my arms round his neck.

'Don't worry, Grandad. *You're* a very kind big man to take me all the way up here, especially as I mucked it all up anyway. I swear I'll be good to Mrs Chummywhatsits. Your job will be safe, I swear it will.'

I *felt* like swearing all the way home. Mrs Cholmondly was not the slightest bit chummy.

Grandad picked her up on the exact *dot* of nine o'clock next morning but she greeted him with a very sharp, 'So *there* you are! I've been waiting and waiting. It's simply not good enough. Well, come along, jump to it now you're here. I have a great deal of luggage.' She paused to draw breath and saw me standing beside the car.

'Shoo, little girl, shoo!' she said, waving her crutch fiercely at me. 'Don't you dare scratch that shiny car.'

'It's all right, madam,' Grandad said quickly. 'She's my granddaughter. She's coming with us.'

Mrs Cholmondly banged the floor with her other crutch, so nearly over-balancing that Grandad had to grab hold of her. She shook him off furiously.

'She is certainly *not* coming with me. I'm not paying an extortionate amount of money for you to give free rides to half your family.'

I looked at Grandad helplessly. What were we going to do *now*? Maybe he should have hidden me in the boot as *this* Old Boot was proving so difficult.

But Grandad could be Mr Smoothie when he wanted. 'I've brought Gemma with me deliberately, madam. I thought she might prove helpful to you. I figured we'd make several stops along the way. She can fetch and carry for you and accompany you to the ladies' room. She's here simply to help you and make your journey as comfortable as possible.'

Grandad smiled at Mrs Cholmondly. Her powdery cheeks and tight little mouth twitched slightly, as if she might be considering smiling back. She didn't go quite that far, but she did summon me to her side with an imperious wave of her crutch.

'Come along then, child. Take my arm and make yourself useful. You can help me into the car but you must be extremely careful not to touch my poor knee as it's excruciatingly painful.'

I felt ready to tug her entire leg off by the end of the journey. She nagged, she moaned, she complained *continuously*. She took up very nearly all of the big back seat so that I was hunched right up against the window, barely able to move, but she still prodded at me to make sure I made space for her poorly knee. I was making space for a hundred *elephants'* knees, but did I protest?

I didn't even mouth a word of complaint when she kicked off her nasty black buttoned old lady shoes and flapped her horrible old lady bunion feet right in my face. I had to help her stuff her warty toes back into her shoes when we stopped at the motorway services. Then I had the most terrible task of all – assisting Mrs Cholmondly in and out of the lavatory.

'Ah, aren't you a kind girl helping Granny?' one lady cooed.

I badly wanted to stuff 'Granny' head first down the lavatory pan and pull the chain on her. Instead I simpered sickeningly.

We drove on, mile after mile. We stopped at *many* service stations because Mrs Cholmondly seemed to have a bladder the size of a pea. We ate several meals, Mrs Cholmondly complaining bitterly at the standard of the food and spilling soup all down her massive bosom. She made me run for paper napkins and help mop it up. I *still* didn't say a word.

'Cat got your tongue?' said Mrs Cholmondly. 'You're not a very chatty child. I like a kiddie to have a bit of spirit.'

'Oh, not our Gemma. She's a shy little thing, good as gold,' said Grandad. He then went into a coughing fit. I think he *might* have been laughing.

When we eventually bundled the horrible old bag off to her poor daughter's house she fumbled in *her* bag for her purse.

'Here, child, this is for your help on the journey,' she said, holding out her hand.

She pressed twenty pence into mine. The price of just one of those dreaded visits to the toilet!

'Never mind, little darling. She didn't give me anything at all,' said Grandad. 'Well, Gem, this trip has been a learning experience for both of us. I've discovered something on the drive back. I'm not sure I like it when you're being a good little girl. You're much more fun when you're being bad.'

Grandad didn't tell on me to Mum about the Cake Incident but she could tell the visit hadn't been a total success. Mum and Dad and Callum and Jack were very tactful and didn't ask any awkward questions. Even Barking Mad sidled round and round sympathetically, the soul of canine tact.

Biscuits' approach was more direct. He came rushing up to me the minute I got into school on Monday.

'How did you get on, Gemma? Did Alice like her cake? Did it taste yummy?'

'I don't know,' I said. 'I was dying to try it but it would have meant licking it off Flora's face and I didn't fancy that.'

Biscuits blinked at me. 'Who's Flora? It was Alice's cake.'

'Yeah, exactly. Only this foul girl Flora got the cake knife and acted like it was hers and so I shoved her head in it.'

Biscuits' mouth fell open. 'You are so *bad*, Gemma!'

'I don't *mean* to be. It just sort of happens. And it's so stupid because I spoil everything. Alice and I couldn't make our birthday wish so now I don't see we can ever stay best friends.'

'Yeah you can. This boy Tim and me are great mates and yet we only get to see each other on holiday.'

'Alice's mum would never in a million years let me go on holiday with them.'

'I bet this Flora's mum wouldn't be too keen either! You are one scary girl.'

'Biscuits . . . you're not scared of me, are you?'

'Yeah, look, I'm shaking in my shoes,' said Biscuits, wobbling about. 'You're the girl who stalked me right into the boys' toilets and wanted to beat me up!'

'I didn't really mean it. Well, I don't *think* I did. I was just a little bit mad at the time.'

'You're *always* a little bit mad. But that's OK. Nobody's perfect.'

'You're generally quite good at acting perfect. How come you're always so *nice*, Biscuits?'

'Oh, it's just my ace personality,' said Biscuits, grinning.

'Well, I don't want to spoil things and make you big-headed so I'll shut up now. Shall we practise our Fat Larry project? You can be him, like I said, and I'll read out the recipes while you demonstrate, OK?'

'I've got a better idea,' said Biscuits. 'We're *both* going to be Fat Larry. Come round to my house after school. Bring your grandad – my granny specially invited him. Just wait till you see what my mum's got for you!'

Seventeen

Biscuits' mum had made me my very own Fat Larry emerald sparkly suit! I clasped it to my chest and danced round with it, the empty green arms wrapped round my neck.

'Oh Mrs McVitie! It's wonderful! You made it specially for me. You're so *kind*.'

'Well, Billy said he badly wanted you to have this Fat Larry suit too, you see. I had the material anyway. I bought yards and yards of it because my Billy's a growing lad and I can't always keep up with what size he is, bless him. It took me no time at all to run up a little mini suit for you. I've sewn in a cushion for extra padding round your tum. You're a little tiddler compared with the McVities!'

I gave her a big hug. Grandad said how very very grateful he was. Mrs McVitie made Biscuits and me special strawberry ice-cream sodas. We scooped up the ice cream with long silver spoons and then slurped up the soda through red straws. Biscuits' granny made Grandad a cup of tea and gave him a slab of her own home-made millionaire shortbread. Grandad said no millionaire could possibly buy better food, and he smacked his lips together, making enthusiastic mmmmm noises. It sounded as if he was kissing someone. Biscuits' granny giggled like a girl, almost as if he was kissing *her*.

Biscuits and I had a slab of millionaire's short-bread too, of course, but we ate it up quickly (but appreciatively), licked the chocolate from our lips, took our gorgeous sparkly suits, and retired to the garden to work on our Fat Larry routine.

We worked and worked and worked on it, day after day. We watched Grandad's video again and again, until we'd got Fat Larry's smile and bouncy walk and catchphrases off pat. We pored over Biscuits' Fat Larry cookery books, mouths watering, picking out recipes.

I had big ideas about a camping stove so we could make crêpes in the classroom but when I had a quiet word with Mrs Watson she rolled her eyes at the very idea.

'I suppose it would be one way of testing the efficiency of the school's fire extinguishers, but I don't think my nerves would stand it, Gemma.'

'Don't worry, Mrs Watson, it wouldn't be me doing the cooking, it would be Biscuits.'

'He's very nearly as accident prone as you are! And if you're within a hundred yards of a camping stove I *know* it would spontaneously combust.'

'You never give me the benefit of the doubt, Mrs Watson.'

'That's very true, young Gemma.' Mrs Watson put her head on one side. 'What exactly are you and Biscuits up to?'

'We're cooking up something very special!' I said, cracking up laughing. 'But I promise we won't do any proper cooking on school premises. We'll have to act like the *Blue Peter* people and say, "Here's one I prepared earlier."'

Barry Baxter did a brilliant project based on the *Blue Peter* presenters, going right back to the days when Mum and Dad watched Peter and John and Val. Barry did it all very seriously, but he had some funny bits too, and he made everyone giggle when he mentioned that naughty baby elephant.

I giggled too, but I started worrying. It looked like Barry might be a clear winner. The rest of the class didn't offer much competition. I was so glad Biscuits had persuaded me not to go for Michael Owen. There were so many footballers I would have kicked myself. Half a dozen kids picked Harry Potter as a hero, saying the same old Hogwarty hogwash till we nearly all went Potty. There were girl bands and boy bands and Justins and J. Los all strutting the same old stuff.

I'd begged Mrs Watson to let Biscuits and me do our project first thing after break time so we'd have time to prepare. We were so busy preparing there wasn't time to eat anything – a first for both of us.

'Never mind. We'll eat our fill afterwards,' said Biscuits, getting all the goodies out of his rucksack. 'Don't you *dare* nick a toffee now, Gemma, or there won't be enough to go round.'

'Just one little lick,' I said, teasing him. Then I looked at the classroom clock. 'Quick! The bell's going to go any second. Let's get our gear on.'

We pulled our emerald sparkly suits on over our school uniform. I combed my hair back behind my ears. We both scribbled a black felt-pen Fat Larry moustache over our lips. Then we beamed and waggled our eyebrows, Fat Larry style.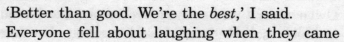

'We're looking *good*,' said Biscuits.

'Better than good. We're the *best*,' I said.

Everyone fell about laughing when they came

into the classroom and saw twin Fat Larrys in emerald-green sparkly suits. Even Mrs Watson laughed until tears trickled down her cheeks.

'You two!' she gasped. 'Oh Gemma! Oh Biscuits!'

Biscuits and I shook our heads.

'We're not Gemma and Biscuits,' I said. 'We're Fat Larry.'

I nodded at Biscuits. He nodded at me.

'Hey, you guys!' we said, in Fat Larry's big friendly boom. 'It's Fat Larry time to give your tums a t-r-e-a-t!'

Biscuits patted his own substantial stomach. I patted my cushion. We did our little Fat Larry soft shoe shuffle, step, tap, step, tap, step, tap, step, kick sideways. I stepped and tapped and kicked with my left leg and Biscuits stepped and tapped and kicked with his right leg, so it looked like we were mirror images of each other.

'Hey, you guys, you're looking slightly saddo. We'll cook you something to sweeten you up,' we chorused.

Biscuits produced a saucepan and a wooden spoon. Mrs Watson twitched.

'Gemma, I said you *couldn't* cook,' she hissed.

'Cool it, little lady,' I said daringly, Fat Larry

204

style. 'It's not like real cooking.'

Everyone craned their necks to see Mrs Watson's response.

'OK, Fat Larry. I'll cool it just this once,' she said, and everyone giggled.

I read out the recipe for ultra-sticky yummy toffee while Biscuits mimed making it with the pan and the spoon. Then he held up baby Polly's toy clock and whizzed the big hand round to indicate the passage of time while I whipped out the big tin of toffee he'd already made. We handed it round and everyone helped themselves, even Mrs Watson.

'Well done!' she said indistinctly, her teeth stuck together with toffee.

'This is only the appetizer!' I said.

'Wait till you see our main course!' said Biscuits.

'It's highly appropriate,' I said, as Biscuits returned to his pretend kitchen at the front of the classroom. 'This is Fat Larry's special chocolate biscuit cake!'

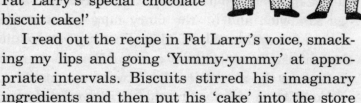

I read out the recipe in Fat Larry's voice, smacking my lips and going 'Yummy-yummy' at appropriate intervals. Biscuits stirred his imaginary ingredients and then put his 'cake' into the store

cupboard, which we'd quickly labelled FRIDGE. I made Polly's clock fast-forward rapidly and Biscuits took the real chocolate biscuit cake out of the cupboard with a flourish. Everyone clapped and cheered when Biscuits got his knife and started cutting the cake into thirty chunky cubes.

Biscuits saved me a slice with extra cherries. The extra cherry on *our* cake was Mrs Watson announcing we'd won the contest for the best project. Barry came second. Biscuits promised to make him a special *Blue Peter* cake as a consolation prize.

'What about making *me* a cake?' I said.

'I'm working on a special cake for you,' said Biscuits. 'Just be patient for a week or two.'

I knew what he was getting at. He was planning on making me a cake for my birthday party. There was just one problem. I didn't *want* a birthday party this year. Every single sausage on its stick and each egg sandwich and all the fancy fairy cakes would remind me unbearably of Alice. I couldn't stand the thought of another birthday cake but Biscuits seemed so keen on the idea that I didn't want to upset him.

I told Mum and Dad (without telling them what

had happened to my last birthday cake!).

'How about a birthday supper instead of a birthday tea?' Dad suggested. 'You could choose your favourite cooked meal.'

'*Not* spaghetti bolognese!' said Mum. 'Anyway, I don't think I could manage a proper cooked meal for everyone after I've done a full day at work.'

'Mum, I told you ages ago, I don't *want* the kids in my class to come to a party,' I said. 'Well. Maybe I want Biscuits. But nobody else. Just family.'

'Callum will want to invite Ayesha. Grandad's coming, of course. And what about Biscuits' family? It's about time we invited them back – his mum and his dad, and there's a baby sister, isn't there?'

'And his granny June! We certainly can't leave her out,' said Grandad.

'That's ten and a half people,' said Mum. 'Where are they all going to sit? And what am I going to cook? Oh dear, I wish Mrs McVitie wasn't such a brilliant cook.'

'She's not a patch on her mum,' said Grandad, smacking his lips reminiscently.

'Pizzas!' said Dad. 'We'll have takeaway pizzas in the garden, with beer for the men, wine for the women and Coke for the kids. Simple! We'll finish up with the boy's cake and we'll all sing "Happy Birthday" to our Gem. Is that what you'd like, darling? You've gone awfully quiet.'

I had a lump in my throat like I'd swallowed a stone. They were trying so hard to be kind to me and make my birthday special. Only it wouldn't work. It wasn't what I wanted.

I just wanted Alice to be sharing our birthday the way she always did.

Dad was looking at me eagerly. They were all looking at me. I had to think about what *they* wanted.

I swallowed very very very hard and got rid of the stone. 'Pizzas in the garden sounds like a super idea,' I said. 'Yummy, yummy.'

My voice went a bit weird and squeaky and I had to blink hard to stop myself bursting into baby tears.

'It's going to be a brilliant birthday,' I gabbled, and then I charged upstairs and locked myself in the loo where I could cry in private.

Eighteen

I woke up very early on my birthday. I waved to Melissa sitting in petticoated splendour on my windowsill. She waved back with her stiff white arm. I kicked my dolphin duvet off and lay beached on my bed, arms and legs flung wide.

'Happy birthday, me,' I whispered. And then, 'Happy birthday, Alice.'

I stuck my right thumb and little finger out, making my hand a pretend phone. *'Happy birthday to us, happy birthday to us, happy birthday, dear Al-and-Gem, happy birthday to us,'* I sang softly.

There was a snuffling sound outside my door. Barking Mad came nosing in to give me a big birthday lick. I patted him and felt a lump hanging from his collar. It was a tiny packet of chocolate drops with a message: *Happy Woof-Woof Birthday, with love from Barking Mad.* His handwriting was very similar to Jack's crazed scrawl. I gave Barking Mad a

209

big hug and then we shared my birthday treat together, one chocolate drop for me, one chocolate drop for him . . .

'What's all this?' said Mum, coming into my bedroom in her dressing gown. 'You know Barking Mad is not allowed to eat chocolate drops. Mind Mum doesn't find out or you'll be in terrible trouble!'

I giggled and Barking Mad drooled.

'Happy birthday, Gemma darling,' said Mum, giving me a kiss.

She handed me a pink tissue parcel tied with a polka-dot ribbon. I shook it for clues.

'Careful!' said Mum.

I saw the word MAKE-UP faintly showing through the pink tissue. Oh dear, it looked like Mum had taken me seriously about wanting to be girly. I tried to pin a smile on my face as I ripped the tissue off. Then I smiled properly, a great grin from ear to ear. It wasn't ordinary girly pink lippy and peach powder. It was a box of *stage* make-up, with all kinds of colour sticks, zingy oranges and crimsons, wild greens and greys and deep blues. I stared at the sticks and saw myself made up as the Incredible Hulk, Spiderman, Dracula, the Lion King . . . My starring roles were endless. There was even a stick of black to make an excellent Fat Larry moustache.

'Oh Mum, it's magic!' I said. I rushed to the mirror to start experimenting.

'Hey, hey, you haven't even washed yet!' said Mum.

'Yeah, well, I'll need to wash *after*, won't I?' I said.

I came downstairs to my birthday breakfast as a blood-crazed vampire, with chalk-white face, purple eyes and blood dribbling down my chin. My school uniform rather spoiled the effect, so I draped a sheet round me, hoping it looked like a shroud. Everyone cowered away from me in a very satisfactory manner. Mum made pancakes for a special birthday treat (she declined my offer of help). I dolloped strawberry jam on mine and pretended it was blood.

I looked round hopefully for presents, even though I had to morph back into a girl and go to school in ten minutes' time. Callum saw my eyes roving and laughed.

'OK, OK. My present's in the hall,' he said.

It was my *own bike*!

'Oh Callum, you're so great! A new bike!'

'Yeah, I'm *very* great, but it's not new, dope. It's Ayesha's old bike. We've stripped it down and painted it up for you. You like?'

'I *love*,' I said, jumping on the bike and trying it out there and then.

'Gemma! Get off that bike! Watch the carpet and the walls!' Mum yelled.

'No sweat, Mum, I know what I'm doing,' I said, taking my hands off the handlebars.

But then the postman thrust a wodge of envelopes through the letter box, startling me. My new bike went whizzing down the hall. I didn't manage to keep up with it.

'Watch the paintwork!' Mum screamed.

'Oh Gem, don't bash the bike up before you've even had a ride on it!' Callum yelled.

I checked the bike *and* the paintwork. For once I was in luck and both were undamaged. I sifted my way through the letters. Bills, more bills, birthday cards from old aunties and cousins and all-sorts. But not the card I was looking for.

I went through the post all over again in case I'd missed it, though I could pick out Alice's handwriting from the other side of the room. I'd sent *her* a birthday card. I'd made it myself. It was like a collage, with photos from every birthday we'd ever had in the past, all the way back to our first birthday when we were sitting in adjoining high chairs with our first birthday cake. Alice was very daintily licking her icing. I had cake all over me, even in my hair, and I was yelling because I wanted another slice.

I'd cut lots of balloons and birthday cakes from Mum's magazines and stuck them in all the gaps, and then stuck a border of silver stars all round my collage. It was all a bit sticky and top-heavy when I'd finished, but I hoped Alice would appreciate it anyway. I hoped she'd like her present too. I'd spotted it in Mum's catalogue, a pink fluffy cushion in the shape of a heart. It was very very pink and very very fluffy. I thought it would be perfect in Alice's new bedroom. It was also very very expensive for a girl with no savings whatsoever, but Mum let me open up an account with her, so I could pay it off weekly. It would take up *all* my pocket money for ages and ages, almost until our *next* birthday, but it was worth it.

I tried not to mind that Alice hadn't sent me anything, not even a card. I couldn't help crying just a little bit when I was scrubbing my vampire face off, but maybe that was because I'd got soap in my eyes.

'Where's the vampire gone?' said Jack, when I came out the bathroom.

'It's daylight so he's flown away,' I sniffed, mopping my sore eyes.

'Pity. Here's a birthday present he'd like,' said

213

Jack, thrusting a black shiny paper package into my hands. When I tore it open I found a black plastic wallet with bats flying all over it, teeth bared.

'Thanks, Jack, it's a cool wallet,' I said.

'Try opening it,' said Jack, as he went into the bathroom to have his ten-second wash-and-brush up.

Try *opening* it? I pulled it open – and found a twenty-pound note inside!

'Jack!' I hammered on the door.

'What?'

'Jack, come out, I want to give you a hug.'

'No fear! I'll have to stay locked in here now.'

'Oh Jack, how come you're so generous this birthday? You're usually really stingy when it comes to presents.'

'Oh, thanks a bunch, Miss Tact and Diplomacy! Actually, I'm not really being generous *this* time. The wallet was a freebie with my *Fantasy Gore* fanzine – and the money's just your earnings.'

'My earnings?'

'All those rubbish jobs you did for me so I'd let you use my computer. I started to feel a bit mean about it. You can use it any time you want, kiddo.'

There wasn't any point now. I was one hundred per cent certain old Cake Face wouldn't feel like passing on any messages.

214

It felt lonelier than ever sitting next to an empty seat at school. Still, I could always turn round and talk to Biscuits. He gave me a great birthday card of a big boy sitting at a huge table spread with hundreds of cakes: iced cakes, cream cakes, cheese-cakes – every kind of cake you can think of. He was clutching an éclair in either hand, taking bites out of both with a big beam of bliss upon his face. The card said on the front I LIKE CAKES – and then inside Biscuits had written, *But I like you more*.

'Oh Biscuits,' I said, blushing.

'What are you giving Gemma, Biscuits?'

'Why has she gone bright red?'

'Show us what he's put, Gem!'

'Hide it, quick,' said Biscuits, blushing beetroot too.

I shoved it into my school bag while Mrs Watson clapped her hands together and told everyone to settle down. Some idiot tried to grab my school bag so I bonked them hard with it.

'Gemma!' said Mrs Watson. 'You settle down too or you'll find yourself in serious trouble, even if it *is* your birthday. Which reminds me!' She put an envelope on my desk.

Mrs Watson had a special birthday card for me! It had a picture of a very fierce old-fashioned teacher with a mortar board and a cane, saying, 'Behave yourself!' Mrs Watson had written inside, *Have a very happy birthday* and she'd drawn herself with a smiley face.

It was just an ordinary old school day, of course, and we had to do the same old boring lessons – but at play time Biscuits and I had a see-how-quickly-you-can-munch-a-bar-of-chocolate competition – and I *won*! As Biscuits' teeth seem to have superior chomping skills to mine I think he might have been chewing deliberately slowly just to let me win.

Grandad was waiting for me at the school gates when the bell went. He didn't just give me a birthday hug, he picked me up and whirled me round and round, though he wheezed a bit when he put me down again. Then he retrieved my birthday present from the pavement. It was Fat Larry's *Special Easy-Peasy Cookery Book for Beginners*.

'You wouldn't mind if I borrowed it off you once or twice, would you, Gem? I'm thinking of asking someone round to supper and I need a bit of help, especially as the lady herself is an excellent cook.'

'Just which someone might this be, Grandad?' I asked, giggling.

'Ah, that would be telling!' said Grandad.

'Might it be a certain someone you'll be seeing shortly at my birthday supper?' I said. 'A certain elderly relative of my mate Biscuits?'

'Hey, hey, not so much of the elderly. The lady's in the very prime of life,' said Grandad.

We didn't go home to Grandad's. We went back to my house to help get everything ready for my birthday supper. Mum was still at work and Callum and Jack were still on their way home from school, but Dad was up and calling to us from the garden. He'd given the grass a quick mow and got out all the garden chairs and covered the mossy old table with the embroidered tablecloth. There was another older tablecloth bunched over something big and bulky up in the tree.

'Goodness, what's that, Dad?' I said. 'Is it going to be a bird feeder for giant eagles?'

'It's my birthday surprise for you, Gem,' said Dad.

He stretched up on his tiptoes and whirled the cloth away, like a bullfighter flourishing his cloak. It was my tree house!
It was a total beauty, with a neat rope ladder and an arched doorway and a proper roof.

'Oh Dad, it's so cool!' I gasped.

I went flying up the ladder straight away.

There was a little notice on the door: GEMMA'S DEN. Inside on the wooden plank floor Dad had put a big fat cushion and a little shelf for my favourite story books.

I couldn't help wishing there were *two* cushions – but I was trying hard not to think about Alice now.

'It's the best tree house ever – and you're the best dad,' I yelled.

I wanted to stay in my tree house all afternoon, but the minute Mum came rushing home from work she made me go and have a bath.

'Then you can put on your party clothes. I've washed your yellow dress and it's come up a treat.' Mum paused. She grinned. 'Your face, Gemma! I'm just teasing. Put on your best jeans and a clean T-shirt, OK?'

She made Callum and Jack bathe and change too, which they weren't very thrilled about. Biscuits looked as if *he'd* just emerged from a piping-hot bath when he arrived, because he seemed extra shiny-pink and scrubbed, twinkling emerald sparkles in his Fat Larry suit. Biscuits' mum was wearing her pink meringue outfit, and Biscuits' granny was wearing hyacinth blue, and Biscuits' baby sister Polly was wearing a very cute little Minnie Mouse dress, bright red with little white spots. Even Biscuits' dad looked colourful, in a purple shirt and crimson tie.

They were such a big bright bouncy family they filled our living room right to the brim. It was a relief, after Dad had got everyone drinks, to spill out into the garden.

Biscuits' present to me was a little Fat Larry glove puppet with short fluffy fur hair and a miniature sparkly green jacket (no trousers because he didn't have any legs). Biscuits made him jump about, waving his arms and waggling his head, doing his own mini Fat Larry routine.

'*Do you like me, Gemma? Am I a good birth-day present?*' little Fat Larry asked me, tickling me under the chin and butting me affectionately with his furry skinhead hair.

'I like you lots and lots, little Fat Larry. You're a truly brilliant birthday present,' I said. 'Please thank Biscuits very much indeed.'

'*Well, Biscuits' mum made* most *of me, but he drew my face,*' said little Fat Larry. '*Biscuits made all of your cake though.*'

'I can't wait to see it,' I said, wondering if it

might be a Fat Larry cake, and if so, whether I'd really like emerald-green icing.

'Well, I'm going to stand back. I don't want you to throw it at me,' said Biscuits. 'I know what you're *like*, Gemma.'

We had the pizzas first. Dad collected them in his taxi. The grown-ups had pretty boring toppings and little Polly didn't have pizza at all, just bread sticks (though she liked these a lot and used them like drumsticks on her fat little tummy). Biscuits and I had a lengthy discussion and came up with a superb ideal pizza: tomato sauce, three cheeses, mushroom, sweetcorn, tomatoes, pineapple, olives, frankfurter sausage and chicken.

'Are you sure that's enough toppings, kids?' said Dad sarcastically.

'Well, maybe we could go for salami too. And beef. And some mixed peppers?' said Biscuits, taking him seriously.

He wolfed his pizza down no bother at all, and insisted he had heaps of room for birthday cake. I had room inside my tummy too, but no room at all outside because there was a severe shortage of chairs, so Biscuits and I ate our multi-topped pizzas squashed up in my tree-house den. We had to raise our arms simultaneously when we ate for ease of movement.

Once or twice Biscuits found himself absent-mindedly taking a big bite out of my pizza as well as his own.

He wanted to fetch my cake and light the candles himself, so we had to do a lot of wriggling and heaving and tugging before Biscuits finally popped out of the tree house like a giant cork from a bottle.

I waited for my birthday cake, my heart beating hard inside my tight T-shirt. I hoped it wasn't going to be a chocolate cream cake like the one I'd made for Alice. I hated thinking about that one now – and the wasted wish.

Biscuits carefully carried a big plate into the garden, candles flickering. It was a brown cake, but it wasn't any old ordinary chocolate cake. It had a little roof! Maybe Dad had tipped him the wink and it was a tree-house cake?

I jumped down to the ground to have a proper look. It wasn't a tree house, it was a cake in the shape of an old-fashioned well. It was beautifully made, every little brick outlined in white, with icing flowers all round the base, and little marzipan frogs and bunnies and squirrels doing a dance around the well. Biscuits had written *Happy Birthday Gemma* in beautiful copperplate icing writing across the well's roof.

'It's a wishing well,' said Biscuits. 'You get the biggest birthday wish when you blow your candles out – and then every single slice has a special wish in it too.'

'Oh Biscuits!'

I darted forward. Biscuits took one step back, looking nervous.

'I'm just going to *thank* you, silly!'

'You blow your candles out first. I don't want the wax dripping all over my cake. Those bricks took *ages*.'

'*You're* a brick, Biscuits, the best mate ever,' I said.

I took a deep breath. I blew hard, and as all the candle flames gave one last flicker I made my wish. I wished that Biscuits and I would always stay best mates – and that Alice and I could still somehow stay best friends for ever too.

I knew it was partly a wasted wish, especially as Alice hadn't even sent me a birthday present, but I couldn't help it.

'What did you wish for?' asked Biscuits, as he helped me cut the cake.

'I can't say or it won't come true,' I said, grinning at him.

'Well, I won't tell you what *I'm* wishing for then,' said Biscuits, grinning back.

We all munched Biscuits' delicious cake. Even

Polly licked a little icing very appreciatively. We all wished and wished and wished.

Then we heard a knock at the front door.

'Is this my tall dark handsome stranger already?' said Mum, giggling.

Dad tutted, pretending to be cross. 'No, it's my blonde curvy dream-girl,' he said. They both shook their heads, smiling at each other.

Biscuits' mum and dad were smiling at each other too. Biscuits' granny and Grandad weren't just smiling – they were holding hands! Callum and Ayesha went sloping off together, holding hands too. Jack pulled a disgusted face and shook paws with Barking Mad, feeding him cake crumbs.

Dad came back through the French windows with a little Jiffy bag. 'It was old Miss Michaels next door. This came Special Delivery this morning and she took it in for us. It's for you, Gem.'

It had a Scottish postmark, though I didn't recognize the writing. I tore the envelope open. There was a little silver paper parcel and a birthday card. It showed two little bears having a big hug, one pink, one yellow. It said *Happy Birthday* up above them in pink and yellow writing, and inside, *Lots of Bear Hugs, Best Friend*.

Underneath, Alice had added,

 Lots and lots and lots of hugs, Gem. I hope you have a very very happy birthday. I'm having a party but it won't be at all the same without you. Mum's made me ask Flora but I don't like her much now. You're still my best friend ever even though I'm not supposed to get in touch with you any more. Dad said he'd send you this, though, in a special parcel, because I wanted to send you something precious. He helped me get the new bit too.

 Lots and lots and lots of love from Alice

x x x x

I opened up the tiny parcel, my hands trembling. It was Alice's silver charm bracelet. Right next to the special little Noah's Ark there was a brand-new silver charm in the shape of a heart. It had four words on it.

BEST FRIENDS FOR EVER.